Advance Praise for Theodore Carter

"Theodore Carter is a silly leaping gnome who dates zombies, practices voodoo, and walks on water, at least when not giggling while making you left-handed, or burning your eyebrows off. Think Roald Dahl as rewired by T.C. Boyle. This first collection of stories is a genre-bending mutant's bible of gross-out jokes and yucks. You will love it."

—Richard Peabody, editor, *Gargoyle Magazine*

"Expect the unexpected—and to laugh out loud—when reading Theodore Carter's delightful and original collection of stories, The Life Story of a Chilean Sea Blob and Other Matters of Importance. Not that it's all laughs; despite their quirkiness, his characters are entirely human, facing their fears around coming of age, settling down, spending life alone, being unloved, or just plain growing old—in short, matters of importance to us all."

—Susi Wyss, author of *The Civilized World*

"We need the fantasies that imaginative fiction gives us to counter the cold truisms that often pass for factual reality. We need modern-day dinosaur sightings, sea monsters, zombies, voodoo dolls, and the occasional upchucked panther for disbelieving therapists. We need these things, this collection suggests, and Carter delivers them to us."

—*A capella Zoo*

"Theodore Carter writes like a (seemingly impossible) mix of Christopher Moore and Raymond Carver. Like a crazy love affair that, in the end, becomes something real and lasting, these stories are both wildly original and gently human. With a keen eye and a razor-sharp sense of humor, Carter tells tall tales about sea blobs and boys who walk on water and 'other matters of importance' in a way that somehow shines a light on the small moments that make us human."

—Dave Housley, author of *Ryan Seacrest is Famous*

"Carter's imagination gives us a holy mess of plots that defy the logic of disbelievers. Something grandiose happens in each story, grandiose and peculiar."

—Zachary Benavidez, editor, *Potomac Review*

THE LIFE STORY OF A CHILEAN SEA BLOB

AND OTHER MATTERS OF IMPORTANCE

THEODORE CARTER

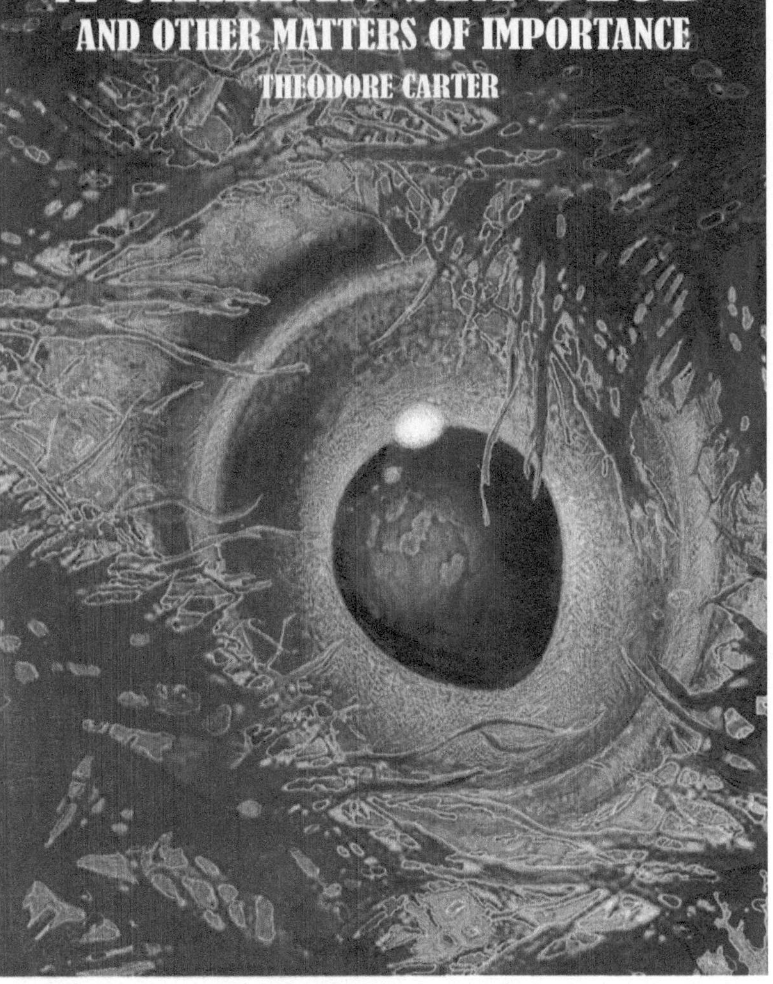

COVER DESIGN BY ALICE CARTER AND COURTNEY GRANNER

AUTHOR PHOTO BY ELIZABETH CARTER

ISBN: 978-1-7327097-3-7
Run Amok Books, 2019
Reprinted Edition

RunAmok

Printed in the USA

THE LIFE AND TIMES OF A CHILEAN SEA BLOB

AND OTHER MATTERS OF IMPORTANCE

For Elizabeth

Table of Contents

The first messengers dispersed from the Lakeview Junior High bike racks promptly at three o'clock and carried the tale of Ralph Buckley's exploits to every corner of the city. A fleet of bicycles powered by strong, sinewy, twelve-year-old legs zoomed along the wide, suburban streets of Lakeview, California, and spread the news in a pattern of concentric rings pedaling outward from the epicenter. Calf muscles relaxed when the children arrived at their respective homes by the hundreds, dropped their bikes on well-manicured front lawns, ran inside, and relayed the story of Ralph Buckley between gasps of air to unsuspecting parents like prepubescent apostles. Becky Shumacher arrived home at three-fifteen. "MOM! MOM! Ralph Buckley walked on water!" she said.

By three-thirty, most every Lakeview Junior High parent had heard the news, and seeing how the event had so visibly shaken their children, felt the need for action. The overarching belief was that this incident was either the result of the Buckleys' inadequate parenting or an act of negligence by Lakeview's principal. In either case, this business about the Buckley kid needed to be addressed quickly. Samuel Dubin, PTA president, penciled it in as an agenda item.

Wanting more immediate action, and fearing the bureaucracy of the PTA, Mrs. Shumacher, Becky's mom,

called Pastor Smith at Lakeview Presbyterian. He urged her to remain calm. If Ralph could actually repeat this feat, if his abilities could be proven, then, said Pastor Smith, he would be able to make a more informed decision about what to do next. Mrs. Shumacher recognized this plan right away for what it was: a stalling tactic.

That very night, Samuel Dubin wrote a scathing editorial questioning the moral fiber of the Lakeview public school system. It was the first editorial he'd written since attacking the teaching of evolution in science class. "What has happened to the moral fiber of our community when children are allowed to mock Christian values and walk on water whenever they please?" wrote Mr. Dubin.

Across town Mrs. Hoskings-Hutchings, known throughout Lakeview as a hippie-liberal troublemaker, wrote her own editorial: "What has happened to the separation of church and state? Lakeview Junior High should not allow this kind of behavior."

The Lakeview Telescope ran both letters Friday morning but did not attempt to describe in an actual news article what had happened Thursday afternoon. Lakeview Mayor Malcom Brown read about the event and decided it would be appropriate to make a brief statement from behind the pressroom lectern.

"While my office is taking this matter very seriously, we have not yet decided what action will be taken as a result of the events that transpired yesterday at Lakeview Junior

High School," Brown said.

That wasn't good enough for the Lakeview Telescope reporter. He wanted a quote with substance. "To what events are you referring, Mayor Brown?" he asked.

"I cannot comment on that at this time."

For each of the past fifteen school years, Ms. Krasner had asked her seventh-graders to prepare an oral report on their favorite animal during the first month of school. It was a time-tested assignment that allowed them to review their research skills, assert their individuality, and get to know their classmates. She'd smile to herself each year as she watched stuttering twelve-year-olds enthusiastically, but nervously, describe black bears, ponies, elephants, snakes, lizards, and the occasional small rodent. She'd written the assignment last August in this year's doormat-sized planner. "Now, I'll give you a few minutes to brainstorm and think of what animal you would like to study," she told the class.

Ms. Krasner was a pro. She wasn't surprised when her classroom became enveloped in chatter. In fact, she thought it encouraging to see such enthusiasm in her students. This year's class was perhaps a bit gregarious, but it could be beneficial. She'd focus on group assignments, team-building, and class discussions. Of course a few of them were off-task already. Ms. Krasner pretended not to notice as Becky and Laura began discussing the chewing gum stuck to the ceiling, dangling dangerously over the teacher's desk. On the other side of the room, Bobby, recognizing an opportune time to make spitballs, began tearing up strips of paper. Becky and Laura would right themselves soon and Ms. Krasner decided not to reprimand Bobby yet. She'd wait to see if he had the gumption to use his artillery. She noticed Ralph Buckley, the quiet, large--footed boy, walking swiftly toward the bookshelf as though fearing a mad rush for the encyclopedias. He grabbed the B volume. Bobby launched two spitballs in Ralph's direction, forcing Ms. Krasner to take Bobby into the hallway for what would be the first of many stern talks.

Ralph felt Bobby's spitball bounce against the back of his head, but decided the incident was inconsequential and brushed his hair with his hand. Ralph had anticipated this assignment and had secretly chosen a topic over the summer. He eagerly flipped through the B volume until he found his entry:

Basilisk Lizard. Found mostly in the jungle climate of Central America, the Basilisk lizard is one of nature's most intriguing reptiles. It is often called the "Jesus lizard" because of its ability to run upright on hind legs across the surface of the water.

He held the encyclopedia close to his chest and felt the titillating nervousness that comes with hoarding a wonderful secret. Beside the text was a picture of the Basilisk lizard caught on high-speed film as it ran across a small pond.

Splashes of water had been frozen on film, the lizard's head tilted toward the sky, its thin, sleek body leaned forward, and its arms and legs splayed in opposite directions. There was no other animal like this. This was the Jesus lizard. Ralph prayed it would be his personal savior from seventh grade academic stagnation.

Everyone, including Ralph, knew he often took school assignments too far. When asked to draw a picture of his favorite animal in third grade, Ralph had spent three weeks painting a giraffe in the pointillism style of Seurat. In fifth grade he was asked to write an essay on a famous scientist. Ralph had started a pen-pal relationship with a Nobel Prize-winning physicist at the University of Michigan.

Ralph's overzealous academic achievement unfailingly spawned resentment from his classmates. Months after Ralph's walk on water, while lining up for recess, Bobby said to Laura, "Ralph, that fucking pansy. Why can't that little shit just do the assignments the way everyone else does?" Expressing his exultation at the new freedoms of junior high, Bobby was perfecting his use of expletives.

"Yeah," Laura agreed.

Ralph's scholastic enthusiasm would have been more easily tolerated if he'd allowed others to write him off as a bookworm, but he didn't really fit the description. Although shy, four-foot-eleven, and years away from puberty, Ralph was a bit of a looker on the seventh grade scene. His tanned skin was a striking contrast to his pale blue eyes. Becky was especially fond of Ralph. "He looks like a young Paul Newman," Becky said to Laura once in English class. Becky didn't know who Paul Newman was aside from his salad-dressing picture, but it was a compliment she'd heard her mother bestow upon good-looking men.

Anyone other than Becky would begin a description of Ralph with his feet. While Ralph stood less than five feet, he wore a robust size-seventeen sneaker. This could have been a cause for constant teasing, but Mrs. Buckley made it a point to buy Ralph the coolest new Nike Air basketball shoes. Instead of Ralph, "the kid with big feet," he was Ralph, "the kid with the cool shoes who also has big feet." Ralph did endure the occasional taunting, but name-calling often digressed into admiration of his tremendous footwear.

Between his handsome appearance and cool shoes, it was difficult for Ralph's classmates to label him as a junior high nerd. Also, no matter how hard they tried to believe otherwise, it was obvious Ralph wasn't trying to show off with his scholarly achievements. He just liked school. This duality within Ralph was his central dilemma. He was a tortured academic who knew that with each new discovery he was removing himself further from his peers. Just as the church placed Galileo under house arrest, Ralph was forced to the fringe of the junior high social scene because of his pursuit of knowledge. Still, he pushed onward and exceeded expectations for every assignment. If Becky Shumacher were to borrow more language from her mom in describing Ralph, she might have mentioned Ralph's James Dean-like allure, a reference to the tortured psychological paradox brewing within Ralph. He was a man of intrigue, of sexy vulnerabilities.

Unwittingly, Ms. Krasner had set Ralph on a course for another academic mania. The day after receiving Ms. Krasner's assignment, Ralph checked out every library book he could locate on the obscure reptile. His real find was a National Geographic video he wore thin by continuously rewinding to the slow-motion sequence of the Jesus lizard running effortlessly over the water.

Standing in his living room, Ralph would imitate the slow-motion video. His mother often walked by on her way to the kitchen and would glimpse Ralph, trapped in a painfully slow cycle of motion, lifting his legs and feet high into the air and placing them carefully down again.

Concerned about her son's self-induced ostracism, Mrs. Buckley tried one day to politely interrupt his research. "Ralph, would you like a snack?"

"Mom, I'm doing my homework."

Mrs. Buckley lingered a moment and watched her son slowly lift his legs, his large Nikes moving toward his chest, and wondered how she had raised a son so out of touch with boys his own age. Perhaps she should consult a child psychologist, or maybe Ralph simply needed more quality time with his workaholic father. If neither remedy worked, she would sign him up for Pop Warner football or Little League next year whether he liked it or not. She had to save him somehow.

Ralph's favorite part of the video came when the narrator, in a deep, authoritative voice, said, "In order for a human to duplicate this feat, he would have to lift his knees to his chin forty times a second. Not to mention the need for webbed feet with a large surface area." Ralph viewed this statement as informative encouragement, not as a proclamation of impossibility. Two weeks into his research, Ralph's report on the Basilisk lizard evolved into a study of physiology and rigorous athletic training. After analyzing various muscle groups and movements, Ralph designed an exercise routine: jump rope and boxing drills for quickness, and yoga for flexibility.

Of course physical training only began after Ralph knew for sure that his body was capable of mimicking the movements of the Basilisk lizard. An exchange of letters with the Nobel Prize-winning scientist from Michigan told Ralph he was at his physical peak for such an unlikely undertaking. Skinny, prepubescent, and almost sixty-five percent legs, Ralph's body was perfect. His fast-twitch muscles were primed, and his joints had not yet grown rigid.

Never again would his speed and strength be in such perfect proportion with his minute mass. "Ralph, this is tricky business you are about to embark upon, but this scientist is behind you. Good luck," wrote his pen pal.

His ludicrously large feet would also prove beneficial. How many times had he heard people refer to his feet as water skis? The put-down now reverberated in Ralph's head as a declaration of his physical assets. His built-in pontoons were a Darwinian advantage far surpassing the Basilisk lizard's mere webbed toes. Yes, his feet were large, yes, they were buoyant, and, yes, Ralph believed that he could run on water. The evidence was overwhelmingly in his favor.

He would have liked to have made a practice run, but the public pools had closed at summer's end, and Ralph feared the private swim clubs would not look kindly upon his unique use of their facilities. The due date snuck up on him, and on October 22nd, Ralph knew that even if he wanted to change his mind, it was too late. The notecards had been written out, and his speech prepared. His research and athletic training had pushed him toward one single culminating event. There was also the matter of having begged Ms. Krasner for permission to deliver his oral report poolside. Sometime long ago, without even noticing, Ralph had passed the point of no return. Still, somewhere deep beyond the reaches of his consciousness,

Ralph had known all along that his research was leading him toward certain humiliation. It was only through practiced ignorance that Ralph could allow himself to bring his discoveries to others and ignore the likely ramifications. He was committing social suicide for the sake of science.

The Santa Ana winds whipped through Lakeview that day. Gusts rattled the chain-link fence surrounding the pool and churned up small whitecaps in the water. Ralph had to shout so his classmates could hear him. He started with, "The Basilisk lizard grows to an average length of four to six inches. It lives in Central America and eats bugs." He fumbled with his notecards, careful not to let them blow away. Nerves caused his voice to waver, and he stammered through his presentation. "Some people call it the Jesus lizard because it can . . . it can . . . ," he turned to his next card, ". . . use its webbed feet to run across the surface of water." The hard eyes of his twelve-year-old peers began to pierce his fragile ego. In the back of his mind he kept repeating to himself habitat, home, diet, and description; habitat, home, diet, and description. He wanted to be sure he didn't leave anything out. It would be tragic to squander weeks of preparation with a bad presentation.

In front of the mass of students stood Becky Shumacher. Her furrowed brow had the dual affect of comforting Ralph, and also exacerbating his apprehension. Ralph couldn't help but think of the note she had passed to him through Laura two days before, "Do you like me? Yes, or no." Becky's beauty was unnerving. Her wide blue eyes watched Ralph in a way he would only begin to comprehend months later. Wisps of blonde hair escaped her ponytail and moved in the heavy wind like rays of sunlight. Ralph stared back at her and continued his presentation, but his brain was elsewhere.

Another accidental shift of his gaze brought Ralph's attention to Bobby, who stared at him with a look conveying both confusion and annoyance, emotions Ralph was certain Bobby would later express with violence. He noticed Ms. Krasner watching him with eyes that seemed to say, Why the heck do we have to be outside for this, Ralph?

Then, suddenly, Ralph found himself reading the tail end of his last notecard. Like a drunk scared into sobriety, Ralph recited his final planned sentence: "Now I would like to demonstrate to the class how the Basilisk lizard can run on top of the water." After pausing briefly in an effort to comprehend the seriousness of his own words, Ralph kicked off his enormous size-seventeen shoes, took off his shirt, and removed his Lakeview PE sweatpants to reveal a tiny red Speedo.

His classmates giggled. Even Becky Shumacher was laughing a bit. "What a fag!" he heard Bobby say. Ms. Krasner yelled out, "Ralph! What are you doing?"

Ralph tried to ignore them. He tried to ignore the cold,

the wind, and his shrinking genitalia as he stretched his legs by the side of the pool. But he could tell his audience was restless, especially Ms. Krasner, so he cut his preparations short. Ralph knew such performances were mental anyway. His prior training would allow him to overcome the physical constraints. It came down to pure concentration.

Ralph stood about ten feet from the water's edge and focused on the fall leaves floating calmly on the pool's surface. He blocked out the jeers of his classmates and checked the string of his Speedo. He sprinted toward the water with his knees pumping high under his chin. Cycles, not force, thought Ralph as he increased his legs' speed, and after just a few stylized steps on hard ground, Ralph's enormous left foot smacked the surface of the water. Then his right foot hit, and he was on his way, plunging and pushing, his success wholly reliant upon one professor's calculations of water density. He pumped his knees high, sending great splashes into the air until he reached the opposite end of the pool and was separated from his wide-eyed classmates by twenty-five meters of sloshing, chlorinated water.

"Coool!" exclaimed love-struck Becky.

"Oh my God, what a nerd," Laura whispered, still unable to believe Ralph had worn a Speedo to school. She hadn't yet comprehended the significance of Ralph's stunt. Ms. Krasner, who many would later say should have been cognizant of the fact that she was leading by example, stood dumbfounded and stared across the choppy waters at Ralph. She uttered her careless reaction quietly, but audibly enough to reverberate through the thirsty minds of her disciples. "Lord, help me. That boy can walk on water." Although Ms. Krasner's words didn't really fit what the class had seen Ralph do, the students nevertheless adopted her "walk-on-water" rhetoric. They'd been trained since kindergarten to follow their teacher with blind faith. Besides, Ms. Krasner's words sounded important, and all the students knew they'd just seen something important.

Many would later blame Ms. Krasner for starting the whole holy mess. She privately agreed that her initial reaction had fueled the hysteria surrounding Ralph's performance. During her years of teaching, Ms. Krasner had learned to become a master of benevolent deception. She had artfully avoided student questions related to religion, sex, and politics on an almost daily basis for fifteen years. She was a master of skillfully incomplete answers and intentionally vague statements. She should have been able to handle Ralph's report: "Thank you, Ralph. Who's next?" or, "Most impressive. Now let's return to the classroom." Almost anything else would have been fine. The only possible rationale Ms. Krasner could devise to defend her outburst was her Catholic school education and her college English professors who'd always taught her to search for symbolic meaning.

This time Ralph's academic achievement did more than simply create resentment among his peers; it created unrest throughout the whole town. If Ms. Krasner had sown the seeds of controversy, then certainly Samuel Dubin, Mrs. Shumacher, Mrs. Hoskings-Hutchings, Pastor Smith, and Mayor Brown helped provide the manure and daily watering. Suddenly, everyone had to decide what exactly it meant when a twelve-year-old boy ran across water. Initial confusion allowed for some ambiguity regarding one's position on the subject, but with the passage of time each member of the Lakeview community was forced to define his or her own stance on the issue. Some willingly accepted Ralph Buckley as a twenty-first-century god. Others blamed physics. Most, however, tried hard to remain somewhere in the middle. They spoke well of Ralph just in case he was part of something larger, but they did not openly embrace his deification.

Pockets of true believers called the radio talk shows to tout their preteen messiah and waited outside Ralph's house to catch a glimpse of him riding his bike to school. Of course there were also those who were opposed to Ralph in every way. They wanted him in juvenile hall and accused him of atrocities ranging from drug use to devil worship. Both of these factions were small in number, but they did a lot to make tentative onlookers uneasy about their relationship with Ralph.

Despite the heavy impact of Ralph's report in the community, it was Ralph's life that really changed, especially at school. Ms. Krasner was far from being a believer in Ralph's sanctity. She'd seen Ralph wipe his runny nose on his sweatshirt and trip over his enormous sneakers too many times. Still, she could not get over the memory of watching him run across the school swimming pool. She was afraid to discount the possibility altogether. Her position was further complicated by the fact that between the hours of 8 a.m. and 3 p.m., she was expected to treat Ralph in a manner acceptable to all of Lakeview's residents. Her job had become a political land mine. As a result, Ms. Krasner made an effort to ignore Ralph as often as possible. This meant a number of changes in classroom procedure.

After October 22nd, Ralph no longer had to take spelling tests. While the rest of the class chewed their No. 2 pencils nervously and tried to remember the saying about where to place their I's and E's, Ralph leisurely perused the encyclopedias. The same was true during math tests. What would happen if Ms. Krasner were to give Ralph a question he couldn't answer? Would the whole town think Ms. Krasner a heathen? Would the dictionary have to be rewritten according to Ralph's incorrect spelling? These were the questions, ridiculous or not, that Ms. Krasner sought to avoid.

Mrs. Shumacher made things worse when she stood up at a PTA meeting and said, "Who is Ms. Krasner to be instilling values in Ralph Buckley, the boy who can walk on water?" Ms. Krasner then adjusted her entire classroom instruction so that lessons consisted only of math, spelling, and grammar. Rules were safe, but ideas, thoughts, and dialogue were too risky.

The community's reaction to Ralph's report on the Basilisk lizard made him even more of a loner. He did enjoy brief star status among his peers for getting into the newspaper, and they generally admired the way he sent their parents into hysterics, but his popularity faded quickly. Many of his classmates were told by their parents to stay away from Ralph. Those who hadn't been explicitly instructed to avoid Ralph did so *de facto* because their friends had been ordered to ignore him. The logic was whether god or heathen, Ralph was a troublemaker.

Ralph's middle school persona was redefined by rumors traded at the snack bar, notes passed in class, and discussions during basketball practice. He became a mythological being who was both feared and admired, but hardly anyone ever spoke to him. By January, when he walked down the halls, groups of children would cease their conversations. Bobby, who blasted "Parental Advisory" music through his headphones loud enough for everyone to hear, turned the volume down when Ralph was around. At lunchtime no one wanted to sit with him for fear of appearing gluttonous while scarfing down Twinkies and Jell-O cups. The only kid who regularly said hello to Ralph was Stephanie Jenkins, a preacher's daughter. Every day she placed a small offering of an Oreo on his cafeteria tray, before moving on to another table.

Ralph found this type of treatment unbearable. The ridicule he'd grown accustomed to would have been preferable. He moved through the school hallways like a heavy-footed ghost, and by spring, Ralph decided his only hope at restoring normalcy was to push Ms. Krasner into revoking her special Ralph Buckley policies through brutish guerrilla tactics. He didn't enjoy disrupting class, in fact he found it absurd, but it was the only plan he could devise to force Ms. Krasner into acknowledging his existence.

Having taken note of Bobby's repertoire of ruckus-rousing techniques, Ralph fired spitballs at Ms. Krasner during the next math test. She sat unfazed at her desk, concentrating on marking the papers in front of her with a red pen. Ralph watched dumbfounded and imagined the internal struggle brewing within Ms. Krasner as she refrained from verbalizing an authoritative ejaculation. Next, upping the stakes a bit, Ralph took a Sharpie from Ms. Krasner's desktop and began scribbling on the blackboard. "Krasner is a Krotchety old Krow," he wrote.

Ralph was not one to scribble graffiti without careful planning. His statement was meant to offend Ms. Krasner on several levels. First, it debased Ms. Krasner's character in a rather pedestrian way. Secondly, the misspellings were intended to jab deep into Ms. Krasner's teacherly instincts, making it almost painful for her to keep from correcting the written statement. Replacing C-s with K-s was a trademark of street gangs rivaling the L.A. Crips. Ms. Krasner could have assumed Ralph needed a teacher's help to avoid a life of gang involvement. Ralph anticipated that perhaps the most worrisome aspect of his graffiti, in Ms. Krasner's mind, would be the three capital-letter K-s easily interpreted as a reference to white supremacy. Lastly, and on the most immature and age-appropriate level, the word "Krotchety" is very similar to the word "crotch." Everyone knew it was unacceptable to discuss a teacher's crotch. Ralph was certain the statement would force Ms. Krasner to act.

Nothing. Ms. Krasner looked at his scrawl, then returned her gaze to her papers. A couple of children looked up sheepishly from their math tests, but that was all. Becky Shumacher flashed him a radiant, devilish smile showing how clever she thought he was to dream up such destructive vandalism, but Becky's grin was a shallow victory. Though he liked to think otherwise, he doubted Becky recognized anything but the most basic maliciousness in his graffiti.

Ms. Krasner was apparently impenetrable. Ralph turned his attention to Bobby. After returning to his seat, Ralph threw paper wads and shot rubber bands at the back of Bobby's head. No reaction. Months earlier, a sideways look would have earned Ralph a few ugly bruises. Ralph turned to the heavy artillery, combining the rubber-band launching device with carefully sculpted paperclips. The first shot was a bull's eye right in the back of Bobby's big head.

With the sting of the aluminum paperclip still fresh on his scalp, Bobby, red-faced and stern-lipped, rose from his seat. He took one fierce step toward Ralph's desk, before Stephanie reached out from hers and grabbed Bobby's hand. "Don't! It's a test of faith." Bobby looked down at her, and his angry expression melted into a look of powerlessness. He retreated to his desk.

Ralph knew it was useless. If he was unable to spur Bobby Gunn into action, then nothing could be done. He was destined to live out his time in Lakeview as an outcast, cut off from communication with anyone other than his parents, who still ordered him to finish his broccoli and clean his room. It was pointless to try to interact with people at recess, and time spent in the classroom was even worse. Ralph hit rock-bottom. He had no friends and had even been robbed of the schoolwork he loved so much. His only companions now were his library card and freakishly large Nike basketball shoes. Even his bike ride to school had been ruined by crazy devotees who lined Pine Road and knelt as he rode past. The only thing for Ralph to do was to count down the forty-three days until summer vacation.

At the end of May, just when Ralph thought he was all

but free from the constraints of seventh grade, Ms. Krasner called him over to her desk for the first time since October 22nd. He scurried over quickly, delighted at the prospect of holding a face-to-face conversation at school. Acting on orders from Principal Haley, who many PTA members accused of spending entirely too much time at church, Ms. Krasner said, "Ralph, now this is up to you, but Principal Haley thought, if it's okay with you, we thought maybe you could do what you did during your oral report as part of the eighth grade graduation ceremony?"

Ralph gave a blank stare. The excitement of just being at the teacher's desk and talking to Ms. Krasner overwhelmed him.

"We could have graduation by the lake this year. And after you finish, you could say a few words. Only if you want to."

Flattered that Ms. Krasner had broken her silence toward him, Ralph agreed. "I think I can still do that. I bet my mom will buy me a new Speedo, too," he said.

Ms. Krasner easily recognized Ralph's desperate need for attention and couldn't help but feel tremendously guilty. She decided not to tell him this was in part a fundraising scheme. Expecting big crowds for Ralph, Principal Haley was planning on passing around a collection box during the graduation ceremony to bolster his state-funded budget. Ms. Krasner watched Ralph turn from her desk and walk out the door with a bounding gait.

Ralph's initial enthusiasm for the upcoming performance quickly eroded into regret for entering into the agreement. On his bike ride home he thought, Isn't this how the whole mess started? He had been asked to perform again many times since his report. Channel Four News had wanted the exclusive. Pastor Smith had wanted a private show. Ralph refused both times, knowing he would only invite more problems. Why now for Ms. Krasner? It was nonsensical. Still, Ralph knew he would go through with it.

October 22nd was the last time anyone had noticed him. They had watched in awe. And although Ralph had become even more of an outcast, there had been that one tremendous moment when he traveled across the water and everyone watched. Maybe this was the only remaining way he could interact with people: as a performer before an audience. If he was doomed to exist in Lakeview in a position somewhere in-between a mortal and a deity, then maybe he should just learn how to behave in that role. He would do it again for the eighth grade graduation ceremony. He would watch the National Geographic video, buy a new Speedo, and do it again.

On June 14th, the crowd watched as Ralph went through a very careful and deliberate stretching regimen on the rocky beach, pulling one knee to his chest, then the other. The eighth-graders, foreign to Ralph, sat in their best attire, and behind them masses of parents and curious onlookers perched on tiered bleachers.

At his mother's insistence, Ralph ditched the red Speedo for a black, full-body wet suit. Mrs. Buckley felt it was more appropriate for such a formal occasion, and Ralph grew to like the way its sheen gave him the resemblance of an actual Basilisk lizard. He practiced rotating his hip in and out and swirling his leg in a circular motion. Each toe had to be flexed and massaged. He'd never had so many people watching him before. It wasn't just the usual graduation crowd of parents this year. Most everyone in Lakeview had come, and Ralph knew it was because they wanted to see for themselves what they'd heard had happened last fall.

Principal Haley stood at the lectern in front of the crowd: "To kick off graduation this year, Ralph Buckley will perform the opening ceremony." Even as Principal Haley spoke, everyone watched Ralph. He tried hard to ignore the familiar faces in the crowd, but he saw them: PTA President Samuel Dubin; Pastor Smith; Chuck Stiltz, the Pop Warner coach; Ms. Krasner; and Leslie Noreen from Channel Four News. "There's a good number of out-of-state plates in the lot," he heard an overweight woman say.

Working to ignore the spectators, Ralph contorted his boyish features into a scowl of concentration. Physics, water density, surface tension, and the Basilisk lizard were all Ralph wanted in his mind. He backed up to where the rocky beach met the dry grass and stared hard at the water. With a violent exhalation, Ralph sprinted toward the lake, his legs moving like jackhammers, knees scraping the bottom of his chin. The water did not stop him. He ran straight across the lake, pushing down with his grotesquely large feet, then pulling them up again quickly, before the water had time to close in around them. Forty times a second his feet pummeled the water's surface and propelled Ralph across the lake in a mode of travel unknown to humankind before October 22nd.

The water splashed around him as he struggled with each step to push himself up and forward, toward the opposite end of the lake. He focused on a tall redwood tree in the distance, watching it grow closer and closer. Just a bit farther, Ralph. He tried not to think about the eyes staring at his back, watching him become smaller and smaller until he was little more than a speck of splashing water. Then, just twenty feet from the bank, he began to feel the bottom of the lake with every plunging stride. Then more soil, and he knew he was there. The water was shallow, too shallow to continue. Ralph had made it across. His chest heaved with exhaustion, and he felt the air burn in his lungs. His feet, immersed, still felt hot from slapping the surface of the lake. He moved slowly out of the water and collapsed face-down on the rocky beach.

"Sweet mother of mercy!" someone yelled from the opposite bank. Then he heard a muffled jabbering drift over the still water.

His face buried among the small rocks, Ralph smelled the fallen pine needles and dry stones, and wondered why he'd done it. Things would be hell from now on, even worse than before. He lifted his chin off the stones and looked into the empty redwood forest, wishing he could just walk into the vegetation. He didn't think he could ever bear returning to the other side of the lake. The water chilled his skin. Why do I do these things? Again the answer came. He had to show that he could do it, that it could be done. He had to prove the narrator of the National Geographic video wrong. He wanted to show his mom that just because he hated Pop Warner football didn't mean there was anything wrong with him. It was physics, Suerat, National Geographic, engineering, and his big feet that influenced him most. But now, lying cold and shivering on the rocky shore of the lake, afraid to look back at the spectators, Ralph felt utterly alone. Just as Becky had missed the complex depth of his graffiti, Lakeview had failed to recognize the significance of his report on the Basilisk lizard.

Seventh grade had been tough, but Ralph tried to remember what his mother had told him, "You are just going through an awkward stage right now. That happens to a lot of kids your age." He knew she was right. Soon he would grow into his feet and wouldn't be able to run on water, even if he wanted to. His pen pal had told him as much. His fast-twitch muscles would develop during puberty, leaving him bulky and grounded. His feet would be of normal proportion to his grown body. That would be the end of it, and perhaps with the passage of time people would forget even something as monumental as someone walking on water.

But hadn't third grade been rough, too? Fifth grade was no picnic, either. Ralph knew he would never imitate the Basilisk lizard again, but there would be other assignments, and he would feel compelled to complete those to the fullest extent.

He heard Principal Haley speaking loudly through his microphone. "Ralph, there is a podium set up on your side of the lake. When you have gathered yourself perhaps you could say a few words to our graduating class."

Ralph slowly brought himself to his hands and knees, lifted his head, and found the podium. He rose to his feet and stood in front of the microphone, staring at the masses of onlookers across the water. He was glad they were so far away. They couldn't see the heavy tears on his cheeks. He was overcome with exhaustion and emotional distress. Standing at the mike, he forgot what he had prepared to say (Congratulations, eighth-graders!) and remembered only a line from his oral report on the Basilisk lizard: "The Basilisk lizard can only run ten to twenty meters on the surface of the water before sinking. It is much better suited for life on land."

EIGHT

Samuel woke with a stomachache, but didn't think much of it until he threw up a live goldfish. Kneeling over the toilet, he watched the fish. At first, he thought the water stirred, not the fish. But when the water settled and the heavier chunks of spew found their place at the bottom of the bowl, the fish still swam around. Its tail moved, gills flickered, everything.

Samuel's nausea grew. He clutched his stomach, staggered to his bed, and burrowed under the covers. He reached for the phone on his nightstand and dialed his boss. After the beep, he said, "Dick, I'm sick and can't come in." He lay for two hours before calling his HMO.

The woman on the phone said, "Five o'clock, but we can only see you in our downtown office."

"Is there something sooner, closer?"

"Sorry, sir. We're over-booked."

"Okay," he said. "Five."

The pain got worse. He began to sweat, so he took off the blanket and lay on top of the sheet. He drank water, but it sat in his gut like strong vodka. The TV screen strained his eyes, and the sound hurt his head. Acid began building in his throat, and he staggered over to the toilet again. Something lodged in his esophagus. He tried hard to bring it up, then tried swallowing it back down. Both techniques failed, leaving him kneeling in front of the toilet, panting, sweating, stomach churning, his head positioned over the bowl. Finally, he threw up. Mostly water, but amidst the spew and bile, a small toad about the size of his thumb swam around.

He called the advice nurse.

"I threw up a live fish," he said. "And a toad."

"What do you mean?"

"I threw up. A live fish was in it. The second time, a toad."

"You ate a fish, then threw it up?"

"I don't eat fish."

"Then how did you throw it up?"

"I don't know."

She paused. "Are you experiencing any other symptoms?"

"I'm nauseous and have a sharp pain in my gut. My head hurts, also my eyes, but I think that's because of the pain."

"On a scale of one to ten, how painful is it?"

"What's a ten?"

"Severe pain."

"Like limbs being torn off, or just really sick?"

"Zero is no pain. Ten, severe pain."

"Eight."

"Intense pain? You'd better come in right away."

"They said I can't until five."

"Did you tell the nurse you were an eight?"

"No."

"Eight or higher, we need to see you right away."

"Okay. I'll come in."

The doctor ruled out appendicitis, then said, "It's probably viral. Or food poisoning from the fish you ate."

"I didn't eat fish."

"Good," she said. "If you're still feeling like an eight after three days, make another appointment."

The next day he woke in intense pain. He e-mailed his boss. His boss e-mailed back: "We sure could use your help on the Freedman grant."

He ate Saltines for breakfast. An hour later, he threw them up, along with a six-inch-long garter snake. The advice nurse said, "The doctor says the symptoms should clear up on their own. There's nothing we can do."

"I threw up a snake."

"Call in two more days if the problem persists."

"I'm an eight," he said.

"I'm sorry."

On subsequent days, he threw up a mouse and a turtle. The turtle scraped the inside of his mouth pretty good as it came up. Sucking ice helped some. He called in.

"The problem persists."

"You'd better come in and see your regular doctor," said the nurse.

The doctor said, "Samuel, I haven't seen you in a while."

"I've been healthy."

"And now you're not?"

"I threw up a live fish, toad, snake, mouse, and a turtle."

"All at once?"

"On separate occasions."

"Oh."

"Is that better? On separate occasions?"

"Not necessarily," she said. She checked Samuel's throat, which was normal, except for the scrapes from the turtle's shell.

"How long has this been going on?" the doctor asked.

"Five days."

"I'm going to refer you to Gastroenterology," she said. "They'll see you within the week."

Over the next seven days he threw up an animal a day, each slightly larger than the one before.

Samuel's boss e-mailed: "I'll need a doctor's note. You've been absent a full week."

Samuel called the advice nurse. "I need a doctor's note."

"I'm sorry," she said. "We have no record that there is anything wrong with you."

"I've been in twice. I have an appointment with Gastroenterology."

"You haven't been diagnosed."

"I'm in intense pain."

"You're really an eight?"

"Yes."

"Are you sure? Does it hurt more than childbirth?"

"Does childbirth hurt more than throwing up a turtle?"

"I really couldn't tell you, sir. Did you tell your doctor about your pain?"

"Yes."

"What did she say?"

"To make an appointment with Gastro."

"Wonderful. I'm sure someone will be able to help you tomorrow."

He e-mailed Dick. "I haven't been diagnosed yet, so I don't have a note."

Dick e-mailed back: "Your absences are unexcused, and we can't pay you for them."

The Gastro doctor poked Samuel's gut, looked inside his throat, and grimaced when Samuel told him about the animals.

"I want you to make an appointment with Mental Health."

"Why?"

"The body can have a physical response to mental illnesses."

"I'm throwing up animals," he said. "Don't you think

that's unusual?"

"Very," he said.

The therapist smiled and motioned him in. Samuel might have smacked her for that smile if he wasn't still feeling like an eight. She asked him to sit, and he did.

"You're throwing up animals?" she said.

"Yes."

"That's a peculiar thing to say, don't you think?"

"Yes."

"Then why did you say it?"

"That's what's happening."

"Tell me more."

"First it was a goldfish. Then bigger things. A snake, and most recently a cocker spaniel."

"Fish symbolize God; the snake, sin. Throwing up is a form of spiritual cleansing."

"But what about this pain? What does it mean? And the cocker spaniel?"

"Are these real maladies or symbolic maladies?"

"Why would I make this up?" he said.

"You're the only one who can answer that," she said.

Unsure how to respond, Samuel stayed quiet. Finally, the therapist said, "I'm prescribing some medication," and handed him a slip of paper. "Come see me in two days."

"Can you call my boss?" he asked. "I can't work."

"Sure," she said. He wrote down the number.

The medicine didn't help his stomach and made it hard to sleep. His boss sent an e-mail: "After speaking with your doctor…long recovery…mental illness…no physical symptoms … highly symbolic … we're going to have to let you go."

He e-mailed back. "Can I keep my insurance?" he asked.

"For a while, so you can get better."

His stomach felt bad when he went back to the therapist. "I'm warning you," he said. "I feel real bad."

"Still with the animals?"

"I threw up an Indonesian anteater this morning. My throat's bleeding, too."

"Are you taking your medication?"

"Yes."

She wrote something down in a notebook.

"You don't believe me, do you?"

"The doctors found nothing wrong with your stomach."

He gave her a dirty look.

"I believe you think you're throwing up animals," she said. "That can be very real, in a sense."

Just then, he started gagging. He knew it would be something big from the way it stuck in his throat. He knew it was a mammal from the scratch of the fur as it traveled up his esophagus and over his tongue. A fully grown panther emerged, slimy from Samuel's insides, its eyes gleaming. It roared, shook its head, then looked at the therapist.

It pounced. She screamed, but her shriek ended when the panther swiped her throat and sliced her jugular. Blood sprayed everywhere. Samuel wanted to be horrified, but all he could think was, *I finally showed her.* The huge cat stood over the therapist and licked at the blood pooling on the carpet. Samuel backed away and tried to leave, but the door was locked.

"Let me out," he yelled at the secretary on the other side of the door.

"No," she said. "I heard a roar and shrieking. I called the police."

"I threw up a panther," he said.

"Fine," she said.

Luckily, the panther had calmed since mauling the therapist. It looked content lapping up her blood and snoozing behind her desk. Samuel watched its tail swish gently back and forth, sometimes smacking the corpse's leg. Twenty minutes later, three cops came through the door. One held a gun with a red dart sticking out of its end.

"Thank goodness," Samuel said.

The cop shot the panther with the dart. It groaned and pawed at the red feathers protruding from its neck, then collapsed. Another cop cuffed Samuel.

"Why are you doing this?" he asked.

"The secretary said you threw up that panther. That true?"

"Yes. Do you believe me?"

"It's rare, but I've seen it before."

"Why are you cuffing me?"

"You're dangerous. What will you throw up next?"

"I don't know."

"Exactly."

"What will you do with me?"

"There's a facility a hundred miles south."

"Can they cure me?"

"That's not for me to say."

There was a trial. The judge determined Samuel's condition dangerous, though everyone agreed it was not his fault. He needed help. The court doctor made a diagnosis. Animalian Regurgitian. The doctor said he'd notify Samuel's boss. Prison wasn't necessary, but they took him to the facility a hundred miles south.

When he arrived, the nurse said, "I think you'll find it quite comfortable," as she showed him to his room. Twin bed. Sink. Toilet. Bars on the windows, which he thought prudent, considering the panther.

"Can you cure me?"

"It's a complicated illness. We can't promise you'll be cured, but we've had some success alleviating symptoms."

"Like throwing up animals?"

"Not completely, though sometimes we're able to reduce the size of the animals our patients regurgitate. With cooperative patients who follow treatments."

"What are the treatments?"

"Medication. Group therapy. Electroshock."

"If it works, can I go home?"

"Most likely not. The symptoms will get worse. One patient released last year threw up a tyrannosaurus."

"Dinosaurs are extinct."

"It was a severe case."

The next day, he met some of the other patients. Compared with the rest of them, he'd thrown up the most vicious animal, and that gave him some status. The facility had a computer room, and he checked his e-mail. He had two. His HMO said they'd received documentation of his diagnoses from an outside physician. If he wanted to be reevaluated by a network physician, his insurance would cover it. His boss e-mailed. He'd heard about the incident with the therapist and the court case and apologized for not believing Samuel earlier. The office had pitched in for a bouquet that would arrive shortly.

Samuel told his story in group therapy.

"It's not fair," said one patient.

"Yeah, but he barfed up a panther that killed his therapist. He can't just waltz out of here and go back to work, you know?"

The therapist said, "Let's not get caught up in the severity of our symptoms. The point is we're all battling our own illnesses."

He agreed with the man who'd said he couldn't be let out, because he didn't think the facility was helping much. He sat looking at the other patients, clutched his stomach, and thought about all that had happened. He still felt like an eight and realized he probably always would.

THE LIFE STORY OF A CHILEAN SEA BLOB

The Chilean marine biologist stood on the beach, her black hair swirling in the wind as she spoke into the correspondent's microphone. Milt watched her on his TV screen from his worn recliner. Over the biologist's muffled Spanish, the English translator said, "It very well could be a new species, a giant squid, or perhaps just a rotting piece of whale carcass. It's too early to tell." A French scientist with a fully funded laboratory had volunteered to run DNA tests. Milt took the bowl of peanuts from his lap and placed it on the side table. He shouldn't have been eating peanuts.

Milt hoped CNN's translation was accurate, that the female voice-over was as precise as possible given the incongruities of the two languages. This was important. Already he was separated from the images by thousands of miles of cables, and his television screen bowed outward-in so he could never be certain of the accuracy of the pixilated images. What if it was all a grand theatrical performance, like *War of the Worlds*? But the running stock quotes at the bottom of the screen and the scrolling headlines assured him this was in fact real. This was news. "This is CNN."

He heard Sylvia rummaging through the pots and pans in the kitchen. "Sylvie, you should come see this," Milt yelled. "They found a blob in Chile."

"I'm not coming out there. I know it won't look like much. That's what it means to be a blob."

"It washed up on the beach. They don't know what it is."

The camera cut away from the marine biologist to the mysterious creature, a gray swirl of lava-like flesh that looked as if it had been poured from a pitcher onto the rocky beach. Men and women walked around the mound of meat with tape measures and cameras. The blob's breadth was impressive, forty-feet wide, said the biologist, but it was only a couple of feet high at most—an animal pancake. The story hadn't earned the "Breaking News" graphic at the bottom of the screen, but the station had given the segment a catchy title: "The Blob: Sea Treasure or Sea Trash?"

Milt had seen the movie *The Blob* on Thanksgiving in 1958. Sylvia had been at home cooking a turkey. Though approaching thirty at the time, Milt had found it easy to forget his age inside the darkened theater and root for the misunderstood high school-aged protagonists. Milt had watched Captain Nemo discover the secrets of the deep in Disney's version of *Twenty-Thousand Leagues Under the Sea*, just a few short years before Sputnik launched the race toward space exploration. *The Creature from the Black Lagoon* depicted a sea monster with human emotions that reminded Milt of a guy he'd known in the army who'd never known the right thing to say. Creature-movie kitsch wasn't so far-fetched. It could even be prophetic.

Perhaps the Chilean blob had a working brain hidden within its enormity, firing synapses to create thought and an awareness of the scientists and beach-goers standing nearby. He imagined a grainy black-and-white image of a handsome leading man standing on the beach in Chile, his face contorted in sheer panic, begging the Chilean biologist, "What does it want from us?" A studio executive was probably already on the scene, asking the biologist to sell the rights to her life story.

Milt yelled toward the kitchen again. "They say they're going to send the blob to a lab to find out what it is."

He could hear the sizzling of browning chicken. Since his last trip to the doctor, Sylvia always cooked chicken——boneless, skinless, saltless, flavorless. She did her best to dress up the heart-safe protein, but her culinary skills couldn't combat the sheer repetition.

"Of course they don't know what it is. If they did, they wouldn't be calling it a blob."

A few years ago Milt had opened the newspaper and learned that by examining a single skin cell a scientist could map DNA. Analysts and ethicists had argued on talk shows about the realization of a Jurassic Park or Franken-stein scenario. Fantastic horrors seemed possible. T. rex might walk down Wall Street or an eight-foot-tall, square-headed monster might ravage suburban homes. But the Frankenstein argument turned into Frankenfoods. The T. rex scenario turned into Dolly the Sheep, hardly a doomsday creature. Soon the whole debate digressed into an argument over stem cells and Roe v. Wade. Here was a chance for DNA research to redeem itself. DNA sampling could turn the blob into an honest-to-goodness sea monster.

CNN's blob segment had lasted only thirty seconds. Coverage turned to war in the Middle East and a story about a canine beauty pageant. At the very moment that Brutus, a bulldog from Athens, Georgia, was crowned canine king, the Chilean marine biologist and the French DNA specialist were probably on the phone discussing the find. Milt pictured the biologist holding a test tube containing a slice of blob up to her laboratory's florescent lighting and looking at it quizzically. He knew the world's ocean experts were contacting one another to ask, "Sea treasure, or sea trash?"

Milt's computer fit awkwardly into the shell of his antique roll-top desk. There was really no place for it. The desk's shelving contained compartments for an inkwell, envelopes, paper, and pencils, but nothing for an IBM. Wiring spilled over the edge of the desk face like Medusa's untamed hair and disappeared into a power strip on the floor. He sat in the black rolling chair ergonomically designed to prevent carpal tunnel syndrome in seniors because, as the salesman had said, "As an older man, it's extremely important to protect yourself against injuries related to computer work." Milt had disliked its comfort ever since. When he hit the power switch, the IBM sprang to life with a melodious chime.

Sylvia must have heard the tone over the sound of sizzling chicken. "Oh boy, here we go," she said. "This blob is going to consume you, isn't it?"

"I just want to know what people are saying," he said.

Though a bit clumsy in its navigation, Milt believed the Internet was miraculous. It could be used to back almost any delusion, hope, or preconceived idea. The lingo that came along with the computer was also a plus. He was now a Web "surfer," an "explorer." While maneuvering his mouse, he pictured himself flying through the world's circuitry in a rocket car, or dodging in and out of a curling wave of ones and zeros on a neon surfboard. Every now and then he'd do something that would crash his Internet browser and remind him of his lack of computer competence. When this happened, Milt pictured his rocket car running into a circuit board wall or himself falling off his surfboard and splashing into a sea of electricity. His IBM (or was it an HAL?) would say, "I'm sorry, Milt, but that's something I can't allow."

This time the IBM hummed along just fine, something Milt perceived to be a coincidence rather than the result of his own actions. After clicking through several short wire stories on the blob, Milt found seamonsterhunter.com. "Sea Monster Found in Chile!!!!!" scrolled across the page in blinking red lettering. Below the headline, plagiarized bits of Reuters and AP stories described the blob's appearance and quoted experts, speculating as to what exactly the blob could be.

According to seamonsterhunter.com, this was a genuine find, akin to the blob that washed ashore in Florida in 1896, but was never officially identified. Seamonsterhunter.com pointed out that mythology from numerous cultures described sea monster sightings. Vikings, pirates, naval officers, and conquistadors had all recorded encounters with aquatic beasts. Over thousands of years seafarers had meticulously reported their sightings in cave paintings, diaries, and journey logs. They couldn't all be imagining the same thing. The blob was proof. Sea monsters did exist. Seamonsterhunter.com had been waiting a long time for this; ever since it launched in 1998.

The discovery of the blob also proved the Loch Ness Monster's existence, according to the site. While Nessie had fallen out of vogue after the rise of sonar, the website claimed that the plesiosaur likely burrows in caves and therefore eludes modern fish-finding equipment. A page of text explained why R.K. Wilson's famous black-and-white photo of the serpentine head was genuine, despite the photographer's recent admission that it had all been a hoax. According to seamonsterhunter.com, Wilson was simply overburdened by the criticism of disbelievers, exhausted from a lifetime of defending his photo. Milt sympathized with the characterization of R.K. Wilson.

Though Milt didn't really believe in sea monsters, UFOs, or Bigfoot, he was still constantly frustrated by the logic of disbelievers.

If R.K. Wilson had only had Sylvia's sound advice to guide him, he probably would have kept his Nessie snapshot safely in a frame on the mantel instead of selling it to the tabloid magazines. Sylvia had recently suggested to Milt that he stop reading his *Ghosts of the Nation's Capitol* on the subway. "Milt, the thing is that people look at you like you're a crazy old man, like they expect you to start talking to yourself or scream at the handrail," she'd said. "With that mess of white hair and your befuddled look, people don't know what to think." Sylvia had spent decades as a researcher for a downtown public relations firm and knew quite a bit about perception. She gently suggested that Milt get his fill of ghosts from Henry James or Shakespeare while on the subway. Sylvia would have given R.K. Wilson some lessons on artful discretion. He would have been better off.

Milt could smell the chicken breasts cooking in lemon juice. With an easy swivel of his ergonomic chair, he looked toward the kitchen doorway and saw Sylvia's shadow on the linoleum. He heard her remove dishes and slam shut the cabinet door, then rustle through the silverware drawer. She emerged from the doorway and began laying down their place settings, her slender hands moving with quick deliberateness, even athleticism. While Milt had grown pudgy through the middle, she'd maintained her sinewy frame and agility, always zipping from one important task to the next. No more weekend tennis or morning runs, but she still moved in the same way. Milt wondered when exactly her curly hair had turned from blonde to stark white, when lines in her cheeks began to accompany her familiar smile. Before Milt could finish taking her in, she'd vanished again into the kitchen.

"So what are they saying about this blob? Is it going to come get us like in the movies? Should we board up the windows and hide in the cellar?"

Sylvia had a habit of starting conversations after leaving the room.

"Not quite sure yet. The scientists are saying it may be some sort of new species, maybe a giant octopus. Did I tell you that?"

"They really think it's a new species? I thought we already had everything neatly categorized and filed away in the Smithsonian."

She was teasing him. For thirty-five years Milt had worked as a curator, categorizing rare items for the Smithsonian Institution. He'd organized national treasures ranging from Abe Lincoln's embarrassing love letters to Jimi Hendrix's dry cleaning receipts, artifacts so bizarre that they were not only hard to catalog, but hard to believe.

"Well, they said it could be just a decaying whale carcass or whatnot, but the scientist, she thinks it's an octopus."

"Remember a couple months ago when that Alaskan truck driver spotted the giant bird?"

"Yeah, fourteen-foot wingspan. Pterodactyl size."

"Well, you thought it was some sort of aviary monster that would irrevocably alter the animal kingdom, remember? You thought it was a holdout from the Jurassic period, but a few days later they decided it was probably just a sea eagle."

"Ah yes, but they never saw it again, thank goodness. The truck driver may have been right. He may have spotted something completely new. It could still be out there nesting on a distant mountaintop, eating small children, or preparing to battle Godzilla."

He heard a snicker from the kitchen, and then Sylvia emerged with a frying pan and spatula. She walked over to the table and slid a chicken breast onto each plate. For a second, Milt could have sworn her hair was blonde again, that it was thirty years ago and Sylvia was young and beautiful, that their kitchen was an H.G. Wells time machine. But then, she reached into her pocket and took out his heart pills and placed them on his dinner plate, and he felt impossibly old.

"Well, I'd bet it was just a sea eagle. I suspect you think as much, but you're just too darn stubborn to admit it," she said.

Sylvia retreated to the kitchen with her frying pan and emerged again to distribute unsalted, unbuttered broccoli and healthful brown rice, hippie rice Milt called it, between their plates.

Milt walked over to the dinner table, took his seat, and looked down at his heart pills. "The Alaskans should make a myth of that sea eagle. Look at the creature economies in the Loch Ness area and in Roswell, New Mexico: Nessie's Breakfast Nook, Monster Mash Night Club, Alien Café, Martian Martial Arts Center. You should get your old PR company on this."

"Yes, radio spots saying, 'Buy a pterodactyl time-share in Alaska. And bring your binoculars!'" Sylvia said.

They'd been to both Roswell and Loch Ness, not as admitted destinations, but because while on a trip to the Grand Canyon in 1982, Milt thought they "might as well" make the four-hour drive to Roswell. Beside the military base's ominous barbed-wire fence, the only other noteworthy stop in Roswell was a small museum filled with crude sketches of aliens drawn by museum staff. Years later, while traveling through Europe, Milt had spent hours figuring out how they could "make a quick jump over to Scotland." It had been more than a decade ago, but Sylvia still teased him, usually while they were on their way to a haunted locale, "As long as we're in the eastern United States…" Still, she had made a sport of it too, buying the worst merchandise she could find at each stop. Her prize discovery had been a compact purchased in Roswell that read "Government Cover-Up" across the lid.

Sylvia came to the table. "Well, I hope this one turns out for you, this blob. Maybe it really is a new species."

"I hope so too," Milt said.

Milt wrapped his arms around the terra cotta pot and carried it in from the garden. His vision was impaired by the plant's stalk, but the three worn wooden steps marked his passing with a familiar groan and told him he was on the right path. Right knee creaking a bit, he bent down and placed the plant deep on the porch, up against the back side of the house where it would be safe from the August sun.

The pain came on almost like a memory, a recollection of his earlier heart failure. First, he noticed he couldn't quite catch his breath. The realization seemed to set in motion additional symptoms. His chest tightened and each breath set off a deep, hollow pain. Dizziness took hold, and Milt sat heavy in a deck chair. The familiarity of the pain was somehow comforting. It made him think he could live through it again. He knew he should yell for Sylvia, but he didn't want her there. Even if he did decide to call out, he wasn't sure he could make a sound. Maybe it would simply pass and he'd never have to tell anyone, just a quiet moment on the back porch that he'd keep to himself. A dirty secret.

The pain grew deeper. His chest felt as if stabbed; the muscles in his neck and shoulders twisted into an unforgiving constriction. Milt tried to replace panic with thoughts about the afterlife, the unknown, the infinite possibilities, ghosts, mummies, but all that came was the thought of Sylvia walking onto the porch and finding him lifeless in a plastic patio chair. His heart was failing. His body was giving up. It was so ordinary.

He was lightheaded, sweating, and saw splotches °of black. Looking out over the yard, his favorite fir tree appeared blurred. He'd fainted once before, and it had been so easy to just fade out, to lose consciousness.

"Milt! Oh my God!" Sylvia said.

Milt looked up and saw her through a haze. She looked beautifully familiar as she stood in front of him, her face frozen in panic. He wanted to tell her he was fine, that he was just tired. He wanted to tell her he was dying. Instead, he said nothing and let her figure it all out.

Sylvia watched as Milt flipped between the only working channels on his hospital room TV: Univision and The Nashville Network. She wasn't sure if the hospital's whole system was on the fritz, or if he was the only patient restricted to Spanish soap operas and professional wrestling. "You only got in here a couple hours ago, Milt. Just behave yourself," she said to him.

Moments later, Milt yelled at a nurse he saw walking past the doorway. It was the one Sylvia had named Ms. Ratched an hour earlier, after observing her large frame and sour disposition. "Can you get this sick old man a ball game on the TV?" he asked. Sylvia realized that in asking Milt to behave, she'd started some sort of game involving the careful prodding of Nurse Ratched.

Sylvia looked at the nurse with a sheepish smile. Ratched's expression didn't change. Her austere, pulled-back black hair looked to have stretched her features into a permanent scowl. "The important thing is you get your rest," Ratched said to Milt.

Milt asked Ratched for the ball game again an hour later. Sylvia knew it was more of an attempt to rattle Ratched than a genuine interest in watching the Orioles lose again. Ratched raised one thinly penciled-in eyebrow and replied, "Can I get you anything to eat?"

"How about a bacon cheeseburger, side of fries, and a T-bone steak for dessert?" said Milt. He'd obviously expected Sylvia to be impressed by his pestering, but she didn't feel like playing along. Sometimes Milt's antics grew tiresome. He was like a five-year-old standing on the edge of the diving board, waving his arms to attract her attention before his next cannonball.

The nurse gave him a scolding look and Syliva half expected her to wag her finger at Milt. Ratched returned a few minutes later and placed a spoon and bowl of Jell-O topped with Cool Whip on the tray over Milt's bed. Milt looked at Sylvia and smiled triumphantly as Ratched turned, her sensible shoes squeaking on the linoleum, and walked out of the room. Sylvia looked down at her lap, trying hard not to show amusement.

"Do you want it? I'm not hungry," he said.

"Thanks," she said, taking the Jell-O off the tray. Sylvia hadn't eaten anything since he'd been admitted.

Upon his arrival, the doctors had told her that Milt had experienced a mild heart attack. He'd need to stay for a few days "under observation." Sylvia wasn't exactly sure what that meant and wondered if they were keeping the more frightening details from her. What did it mean to have two heart attacks? Is the damage cumulative?

She relayed what she'd been told to Milt who acted as if he were on some twisted, Kafkaesque vacation where he could break from life's daily duties, but was subject to medical procedures. "So I guess this is what it feels like to be 'under observation,'" Milt said. "What do you think, Sylvie; will nurse Ratched look over my body with a magnifying glass? Or maybe the observation is done with a hidden camera somewhere in the room. Perhaps Ratched is an agent of Big Brother. Next time she'll come in wearing a pea-green military uniform and wielding a state-issued thermometer. Perhaps the limited television is part of her propaganda war, an attempt to make me into a new breed of eighty-year-old, Spanish-speaking pro-wrestler."

Sylvia sat hunched in her chair and studied the movement of her hands as she ran her fingers over a leaf she'd picked off a plant in the lobby. "I suppose they're going to check your arteries and your heart valves to make sure everything is okay."

It was silent for a moment. Silence had always unnerved Milt. "You've been observing me for over fifty years," he said. She didn't know what it was supposed to mean, but understood he was thanking her for something.

Sylvia kept her face pointed toward her lap. "Yes, long enough to know you're a crazy old man. You can't lift a seventy-five-pound potted plant like you did when you were twenty-five. You shouldn't do things like that, Milt." She'd started several conversations like this since his first heart attack, and they always ended badly. While Sylvia accepted the predictable onset of arthritis and liver spots, Milt always looked as if he felt betrayed by what he saw in the mirror.

Sylvia, in part thankful he chose to ignore her statement, turned toward the television and pretended to be engrossed in the muted fishing show. After a few minutes, Milt turned off the TV. She realized the predictability of watching overweight men reel in only one kind of fish was likely torturous for him. He'd probably have preferred they catch an old shoe or a rabid muskrat.

He lay still, looking up at the square tiles on the ceiling. "Hey, Sylvie," he said. "Remember that sea blob from yesterday? Did the lab results come back from France?"

"I picked up a paper in the gift shop this morning," Sylvia said. She reached under her chair, pulled out the newspaper, and turned to the back page for the minuscule wire story she'd noticed about Milt's sea blob.

Sylvia was about to read the article word for word, but Milt was sitting up expectantly. He clenched the edge of his blanket in two balled fists, and his eyes grew wide in anticipation. She couldn't bear to send him back to muted bass fishing or to watch him study the ceiling. What Milt liked more than anything was to drive her into mischievousness. Sylvia tried hard to suppress a smile, but a smirk snuck out anyway, which may have given her away, but it hardly mattered.

"It says here that in order to perform accurate tests, the Paris laboratory asked that the entire blob, not just a portion, be transported from Chile to France. The creature was loaded onto a barge using a specially designed crane constructed by a Chilean engineer in just two hours." She paused and looked at Milt to see if he'd stop her. He didn't.

"While making its way around Cape Horn, the ship was h̆acked by South Asian pirates. Apparently, when the pirates saw the armed guards on the barge's deck, they assumed the ship was carrying precious metals. After a shoot-out with the armed guards, the pirates found nothing in the cargo hold but the giant blob. They were so upset they took over the entire barge. So the blob never made it to France. A South Asian pirate gang is toting it around the Atlantic. The National Academy of Sciences is furious about the loss of this important specimen and has hired a mercenary naval fleet to meet the pirate-controlled barge for battle off the coast of Brazil. So, we should know more later." Then, deciding an extra bit of detail was needed for authenticity, she added, "Oh, it says here the name of the barge is 'Nautilus.'"

"Ha!" said Milt, clapping his hands. "That's great. A sea monster captured by pirates. We'll have to see how this turns out; see if the NAS can win back that sea blob."

Milt's IV bag jiggled on its metal stand. His sudden movement had pulled at the slack in the plastic tubes hooked into his arms. Sylvia stood up to make sure nothing had dislodged.

"I'm allowed to move, Sylvie. The tubes are stuck in there. Tomorrow I may go for a jog."

Sylvia awoke from a night's sleep in the bedside chair to start Milt's second day of observation. Nurse Ratched came in soon after to check Milt's vitals and fluids and wrote things on a clipboard. They talked about her for a while after she left, then about how Milt would be better soon, but that was about it. He looked ashamed tucked into his standardized bedding, machines beeping, nurses scurrying in and out and talking in sterile language and necessary pleasantries. Milt had been so quiet Sylvia started to worry that his second heart attack had clogged up a bit of his quirk. Their second day in the hospital was only bearable because every few hours he would ask her for the latest on the sea blob.

Sylvia felt relieved at having a duty to perform. She

would take the newspaper, now a day old, out from under her chair and give Milt the news. The NAS mercenaries had been victorious after a six-hour battle during the night. Still, the blob had not been transported to the laboratory because it had started to melt while traveling by truck toward Paris. It was being temporarily stored in a meat locker somewhere in the French countryside.

Sylvia knew the conclusion of the blob saga would have to coincide with Milt's release from the hospital at noon the next day. Two hours before his release, Sylvia wracked her brain for an ending. The Chilean biologist, the heroine of the story, had finally overseen the successful transport of the blob to the Paris laboratory and received the results, which of course showed the blob is indeed a new species. The saga would conclude with Sylvia's next installment. There were papers to sign and things to gather before noon, but that would be the easy part of getting Milt home. With just a half-hour to go, Milt acted coy and asked, "So Sylvie, what's the latest on the blob?"

Sylvia opened the newspaper and held it up in front of her. "The scientific community is in awe of the complex DNA coding contained in the mysterious blob, now officially named *blobous amorphous*," said Sylvia. "Officials are just beginning to understand the medicinal potential of this new species; however, they've already found that proteins from *blobous amorphous* can be used to extract cholesterol from cheeseburgers, potato chips, and peanuts. Chilean biologist Elsa Acosta will no doubt receive the Nobel Prize for finding what will likely become the miracle cure for heart disease. Conservationists have already agreed to fund research that will examine how scientists can grow *blobous amorphous* specimens in a laboratory setting and curb over-fishing of the now wildly valuable and highly elusive animal. The president of the United States is scheduled to speak later today . . . "

Sylvia laid the paper on her lap and looked at Milt's deeply wrinkled face that'd grown a bit sallow over the last few days. He looked sick, and the hospital room was barren and sterile. She wanted to tell him what had really happened.

She knew from his worried look that he had an idea of what was going through her mind. Waving his hand, he said, "No, no, you're doing fine. Keep going."

"But it's all been resolved. The DNA results came back from the lab yesterday."

He grimaced, and waved his hand at her again. "You're doing fine. Go on, Sylvie."

She kept looking at him and curled the newspaper in her hands. "Milt, this is nonsense. The doctor says it was just a mild heart attack. You're really doing just fine, Milt. You don't have to worry. You'll be fine for quite some time."

"Sylvie, what does it say about the captured pirates? When is the trial?"

She realized they could only go on like they had for fifty-five years. She lifted the paper to hide her eyes. Her voice grew shaky. "The International Anti-Piracy Commission has asked that the trial be held in the United States. They want the blob-nappers prosecuted to the fullest extent of the law. They say there is nothing more serious than endangering the life of a newly discovered sea monster. No one should ever do it." She folded the paper, placed it in her lap, and looked at Milt.

"Perfect, Sylvie."

His eyes were closed and his head titled back on the pillow as if he were inhaling the fumes of a fine cigar. Still seated, Sylvia leaned forward, reached out, and closed her hand around Milt's little finger.

I USED TO LOVE HER

She saunters out through the bedroom doorway naked, stiff-legged, her neck bent to the side, moving in a series of jerks.

"Sara, you all right?" I ask. We've been fighting recently. I want to sound concerned.

"Yeah, okay," she says, but her voice is gravelly, barely comprehensible, filled with phlegm. I leave her alone as she squeezes past me into the bathroom and closes the door.

We left the bar at 3 a.m., bickering because some stranger had tried to kiss her and nibble her neck. "Maybe I should have let him," she said, as we stumbled drunkenly into a taxi.

"Maybe you did," I replied.

We spilled out of the cab and made it up the steps to our front door with the help of the sturdy handrail.

Behind the bathroom door, I hear her making a hacking sound. It could be a cough, vomiting, I'm not sure. She gets pretty uptight about me being around when she's like this. She has antiquated ideas about looking "fresh," so I leave her upstairs and go down to the kitchen to make breakfast. I hear the shower running.

She comes into the kitchen wearing my old, blue T-shirt, and a pair of mesh shorts. An odd choice, but I like that she's wearing my shirt. Maybe we've made up. The shirt's neck pulls to the right, the waistband on her shorts is askew, and her underwear hangs out on one side, but not in a sexy way. She looks haggard. Death warmed over. Her normally pale skin is almost blue, and dark; purple bags show under her eyes. I should say something kind, reassuring. I pull out a skillet from the cabinet. "Do you want some eggs?"

She grunts in affirmation and scratches her scalp. Her wet, brown hair falls in front of her face. I turn and work at the stove, pretending to labor over the eggs. She really looks like hell, and though I know it's petty, I'm pretty disgusted. I try to push such immature thoughts away. Sara is my first long-term relationship, my first go at commitment, and I shouldn't fuck it up because she looks like crap when she's hungover. I'm past that. I think I'm even in love with her.

I push the eggs around in the pan, and get a whiff of something acrid. I take the pan off the heat and smell it. Maybe the eggs are bad. It isn't the eggs though, and after a moment I begrudgingly come to the conclusion that the smell is Sara. I turn and look at her over my shoulder. She's sitting on one of the barstools at the counter, swaying back and forth like Stevie Wonder. She looks at me and makes a slow, guttural grunt. I turn back to the eggs. Jesus, she's disgusting. If it weren't for her wet hair, I'd find it hard to believe she actually got in the shower.

I know there are times when I come home looking like

shit, or I play hoops and don't shower right away, and Sara never says a word. It's ridiculous for me to be so shallow. I start thinking about all the things she does that annoy me, how she leaves the peanut butter knife out after making a sandwich, how she picks at her toenail polish when we watch TV. Stuff like that.

"Here are your eggs," I say, and I slide the plate and a fork in front of her. She grabs hold of the fork with her fist and starts stabbing at her eggs. When I went to her parents' house for Thanksgiving, they had about four forks at each table setting. I can't believe this is the same girl those people raised. I figure, you know, sometimes when you're hungover, your whole body feels weak. Your arms feel heavy. She wouldn't give me grief for it, so I leave her alone. I stand at the counter across from her and eat my eggs, but can't help watching. She only stops momentarily to look at the gurgling coffee maker with quiet skepticism, then she's slurping down her eggs again like she's eating a bowl of soup. Half of the eggs aren't even going into her mouth. She's like Cookie Monster, her food dribbling down her chest and onto the floor.

"So, how you feeling?" I say. She hasn't really said anything to me since she woke up, and I wonder if she's still mad. She doesn't answer, only shifts her wary gaze back toward the brewing coffee.

The coffee machine beeps, signaling it's ready. Sara pops out of her seat. She looks at me briefly before walking over, with the same laborious gait, to the coffee pot, and swiping it off the burner with a backhanded slap.

"RAAAAAAAAAAAARRR!"

"Jesus Christ, Sara!" But I sure as hell don't want to fuck around with her if this is how she's going to act, so I don't say anything else. She stumbles out of the kitchen and through the front door, letting the screen door bang shut behind her.

I let her go. Maybe this is best, for her to leave for a while. When she comes home, she'll approach me with her head down, then look up at me with those soft eyes, and give me an apologetic hug. Still, I have to get the mop out for the coffee and sweep up the glass shards. It's hard not be angry.

I hear her an hour later. She lets the screen door bang behind her again as she enters. Instead of the soft, forgiving look I was expecting, she growls and walks past me into the kitchen. Her skin is a deeper blue-purple tone now, and I can see the outlines of her veins like spiderwebs on her cheeks. This has to be something more serious than a hangover.

"Sara, you feeling okay?" I say. She only grunts.

Her bare feet are muddy, and I'm thinking it's good I haven't put the mop away, but I'm worried, while she goes into the kitchen, as to whether I've cleaned up all the glass. If she cuts her foot, she's likely to bite my head off.

I study the brown footprints she left on the carpet. The

markings are tinged with red. I look out the front door and see a dead cat on our front steps, a pool of blood underneath its carcass, its neck bent at an unnatural angle. A neighborhood dog or raccoon probably got to it, I think, though I can't be sure.

I go into the kitchen. Mindlessly, Sara paces back and forth. Drooling. Grunting. "We should take you to a doctor," I say, but it is Sunday, and there's no way in hell Sara is going to let me drag her to urgent care.

She doesn't respond, only moves toward me with that painful-looking walk. She holds her arms out in front of her, her head bent to the side. A strand of spittle runs from the corner of her mouth. I think maybe she's approaching me for the apologetic hug I predicted. I smile and reach out, trying not to show my hesitation, my wincing at her deathly blue skin, her rotten smell, her uncontrolled drooling.

We embrace. I grab her around the back and squeeze. She feels sweaty, fleshy, rigid like a piece of boney fish. As I hold her, I think, that's it; I need to break up with her, if not today, then soon. I've felt this way before, but then settled down.

She leans into my neck and tries to bite me.

"Sara, stop!" I say, but she does it again.

I push her away, and she snaps at my finger with her teeth. She misses, and her jaw smacks closed with a loud cracking sound. She snorts, letting out horrid-smelling breath so foul I wonder if she bit that dead cat, broke its neck with her teeth.

"Stop!" I yell.

Sara can be pushy, really bossy. She's never acted this badly before, but she does have a temper. She stands in front of me, her face contorted into an ugly scowl. This is when I get fed up. I can understand up to a point, but the truth is, she's been in a foul mood a lot lately. I know relationships are about compromise, but she's a real drag.

I look at her in silence as she approaches. She's still grunting softly. Maybe I'm not in love with her anymore, just wanting to be. She never lets me pick the movie at Blockbuster, never wants to eat out at my restaurant choices, never wants to hang out with my friends. She's always making snide remarks about my clothes, saying things like, "Let's go buy you some more nice pants." The bars she likes charge five-fifty for a Corona. Whenever she borrows my car, she takes my Guns N' Roses out of the CD player and leaves in Tori Amos. It's comforting to finally realize her selfishness, but I can't ponder it too long because she's stumbling toward me.

"I need some time to think," I say, but she doesn't seem to hear. I scamper past her and out the front door. The neighborhood is quiet, almost eerily so, but it helps me think. After a few blocks, I become even more certain. Sara's not right for me. Not anymore. Commitment is good. I can commit, but I shouldn't commit to Sara. I deserve someone kinder.

It feels good to come to this conclusion on my own. I think it helps me act with a clear head later when she starts eating the raw meat out of the fridge and going after small animals in the yard.

"Sara, I'm sorry," I say as she lumbers across our cement patio, knocking over a lawn chair in an attempt to swipe up a blue jay she's wounded. "I've got to call someone. You're out of control." She's focused on the elusive, fluttering jay.

The operator says all ambulances have already been dispatched. "A busy day," she says, and as she's saying it I realize I can hear multiple sirens in the distance. She promises to send the cops.

I'm on the front steps when the squad car screeches to a halt in our narrow driveway. A big, mustachioed patrolman gets out, holding a shotgun.

"Where is she?" he asks.

I notice the right sleeve of his uniform is torn and there is a smattering of blood on his thigh. "Out back," I say, pointing.

He pushes past me into the house. I follow as his heavy boots shake the floor. He stops while exiting the sliding glass back door and stands with one foot in the kitchen, the other on the top step like he's afraid of getting too close. "Stand back," he says, and he points his shotgun at her.

"Wait!" I yell, but he ignores me and lifts the gun, taking aim. Everything is happening so fast. I want to talk things through.

Sara takes a slow, but aggressive step toward the cop, bares her teeth, and hisses.

"Sara, please," I say.

The gun gives a monstrous roar, and Sara's head is nearly blown clean off. It's devastating. I scream in horror as her blood spills over the patio. Still, at least I know it never would have worked between us.

Jed took the package from the UPS man, looked at it quizzically, and studied the sloppy scrawl on the address label.

"You expecting something good?" the deliveryman asked.

"Not expecting anything," Jed said, his eyes still focused on the box.

The deliveryman shoved the electronic signature pad under Jed's nose.

"Sign here, please."

Jed pinned the package to his side with his elbow, accepted the electronic clipboard, and hurriedly signed his name.

"You seem pretty excited," the UPS man said.

While handing back the clipboard, Jed looked at the man's face for the first time and noticed a toothy grin underneath his brown mustache. The UPS man was teasing him, it occurred to Jed, and he wondered why he so often found himself the subject of ridicule.

Jed shrugged his shoulders. "I guess so," he said. The UPS man didn't speak, but looked down at his clipboard, gave a nod of approval, then turned and walked toward the elevator.

Not many people knew his new address. Jed thought it likely his mother had found some childhood relics while cleaning out the attic. He felt the weight of the box to see if it could be a stack of his old rodeo magazines, or perhaps his bottlecap collection, but the shape and weight didn't seem right for either.

Jed considered it a small triumph when a situation dictated that he reach into his pocket and pull out his Swiss army knife. Even now, alone in his small apartment, he felt impressive as he rolled up the sleeves of his flannel shirt and used his handy knife to cut through the packing tape.

The box was chock-full of newspaper, more specifically, the sports section of the New Orleans Times Picayune. He didn't know anyone in New Orleans. Beneath the crumpled newspaper lay a hideous humanoid figure constructed from what looked like refuse. The figurine's head was a crude, clay skull molding, complete with strands of dried-out hair. The doll's mouth was filled with a row of teeth aligned behind a lipless grin. Broken sticks, old chicken wire, and long strands of bristly hair intertwined within the twisted construction of its limbs. It wore bright orange pants, and a rather elegantly sewn black felt jacket complete with colored plastic gemstones, white trim, and buttons. Jed knew the bizarre gift had to have come from Roy, his freshman roommate. There was a card, or more accurately, a torn slip of a diner menu with writing atop the list of à la carte breakfast items. Roy had written:

> JED,
>
>   A GENUINE VOODOO DOLL FROM NOLA. CREEPY, HUH?
> OFF TO HOUSTON NEXT. MAYBE I'LL FINALLY SEE A
> RODEO.
>   SCOOTER

Scooter was a name bestowed upon Roy in college sometime after his freshman year. Jed didn't know the significance or origin of the nickname, even though Roy seemed to think he did. Hopelessly friendly and loyal, Roy didn't seem to remember that he and Jed hadn't talked much after freshman year. Their pairing had been an awkward match; it could only be explained by the humor the student housing office must have intended by coupling Jed, a cattle ranch kid from Gilroy, California, with Roy Gill, a suburbanite from the Santa Monica area.

Roy had taken a job with a management consulting firm after graduation, which meant he traveled to a new city every few weeks. While Jed didn't even know Roy's phone number or mailing address, Roy would periodically send Jed postcards from various U.S. cities. A postcard had arrived a few months earlier from Miami Beach, depicting a metallic badge that read, "Official Thong Inspector." A postcard from Seattle had shown the fish market. Now, here was the voodoo doll from New Orleans.

Whenever he received these mementos, Jed thought of

new reasons why his position at the Wild Horse and Burro Division of the Bureau of Land Management, Bakersfield Field Office, was more important than management consulting. While sitting in his cubicle and calculating the amount of public land needed for a population of wild ponies, Jed considered himself a white-collar cowboy. He didn't understand management consulting but got the sense it meant putting on a nice suit and weaseling companies out of revenue. He imagined Roy would be very good at a job like that.

Jed turned the doll over in his hands, looking for some clue as to its utility. There was no hook on the back to suggest it should be hung on the wall, no attached card describing its historical significance, and no instructions for ceremonial use. But, because it was a gift, Jed couldn't bring himself to throw it away, despite its hideousness.

His sparse studio apartment left only a few options for display. Aside from his futon bed, the center of his decorating scheme, Jed's only other furniture was a bureau and a small table on which he'd placed an old TV. He put the doll on his dresser, propping it against the wall in a standing position next to his wallet, keys, and boom box.

The doll's orange pants and gemstone jacket buttons looked especially garish. It was the only ornamental item in the room aside from the BLM lands map tacked over the bed. Despite its twelve-inch stature, the colorful figurine was now the focal point of his colorless apartment, its expression suggesting a gregarious and mischievous personality.

Jed felt a bit embarrassed as he undressed in front of the doll while preparing for bed. There was something unnerving about its representation of animate life. He took one last look into the carved sunken eyes and wide grin of the misshapen clay head, before turning off his bedside lamp. Why had Scooter thought he'd be interested in such a grotesque piece of folk art?

As morning sunlight filtered through the Venetian blinds, Jed woke to find his voodoo doll pacing on top of his dresser, one hand (or stump) held close to its head as if holding a phone, the other gesticulating in grandiose motions. Jed knew from his own experience, and from stories told by others, that upon waking it is not uncommon to confuse a dream with reality. This knowledge was not at all comforting as he watched the doll's gestures become more emphatic. The figurine was obviously irate over something, and Jed flinched as it suddenly slammed the invisible phone into its nonexistent receiver.

Afraid to move, Jed sat in bed and watched the doll walk over and sit on his cowhide wallet, reach into its coat pocket, tilt its head to the side, put both arm-ends up toward its mouth, and tilt its head back in a mock exhalation. The figure stared off into the corner of the room opposite Jed and took periodic puffs off an imaginary cigarette.

Jed wiped the morning grogginess from his eyes but still saw the doll moving its left arm up to its mouth. He tried to figure out what had happened to create such delusions. Had he added spoiled milk to last night's mac n' cheese? Had some hallucinogen been mixed into his toothpaste? Had Scooter's package contained mind-altering pixie dust he'd inhaled while rummaging through the crumpled newspaper?

As the doll stubbed out the cigarette, Jed grew hopeful that some sort of mechanical device lay inside its twig construction. He grabbed the doll off the shelf, its body turning rigid in his hand. He pulled it close for a more thorough examination, but found nothing that would suggest the joints or motors necessary for movement. Jed even sheepishly lifted the doll's jacket and pulled down its pants in hopes of finding answers. Discovering nothing, Jed put the figurine back on his dresser.

Now finished with its cigarette, the doll began miming a new action. It removed its jacket and pants to reveal its svelte twig body. It tilted its head back, ran blunt arm-ends through stringy, dried hair, and then rubbed its armpits. And because there was nothing else he could do, Jed decided he would step into the shower and get ready for work. He hoped to regain whatever mental capacity he'd lost during the night by following his predictable morning routine. Aside from the moving doll, everything was as it had been the day before. Physically, he felt fine.

Dressed and ready for work, Jed took a few minutes to watch the doll. It was completely still, balanced on his bureau. As he sat on his bed staring, Jed felt as ridiculous as when he'd thought the doll had come alive. "Is that it, doll?" he said. "No more action?"

Motionless, the doll peered back with vacant eyes and its toothy grin. Unwilling to give credence to what he'd seen earlier, Jed left his apartment, got into his pickup, and drove to the office.

Each day, as Jed sat in front of his government-issued computer, he reminded himself that the (federal) taxpayer paid his salary. It was only fair he conduct his analysis of wild horse and burro grazing lands with Neilimum efficiency. This meant the Internet was strictly a workplace tool to aid in his implementation of the Wild Horse Act of 1959. Numerous department memos had said as much. Still, after watching his voodoo doll hold a phone conversation, smoke a cigarette, and take a shower, Jed couldn't resist spending the entire day attempting to learn everything he could about New Orleans voodoo. Though he tried to convince himself he hadn't seen anything, he rationalized his research as cautionary background information, just in case.

He'd exhausted the most credible sites by midmorning —web pages of voodoo shop owners, Vodun priests, and historical accounts. Even the pages written by the most devout believers said nothing about voodoo dolls coming to life. Desperate for some viable explanation for what he may have seen, Jed ventured onto fringe web sites that seemed less about voodoo than about all things bizarre and grotesque, including one site featuring photos of roadkill. He pulled his rolling chair as close to his computer as his fiberboard desk would allow and leaned in toward the screen in an unsuccessful attempt to hide his web wanderings from coworkers.

Jed was startled by the sound of Randy's voice over his shoulder. "Woah, Cowboy, what you looking at there?" Randy had given Jed the "Cowboy" moniker Jed's second week on the job after he'd worn a larger than average belt buckle to secure his casual-Friday jeans. Jed swiveled in his chair and saw Randy leaning against the file cabinet, his trademark American flag coffee cup in hand. Randy's voice always made Jed wish he were elsewhere, and this day his coworker's presence was especially troubling. Randy had already noticed Jed's non-work-related Internet use; Jed envisioned his name in the 2004 Inspector General's report on government waste, fraud, and abuse.

Randy placed his coffee mug on the cabinet, put his left hand on Jed's desk, and leaned in for a look at the screen. Jed could smell his coffee breath. Randy wrinkled his sun-stiffened brow as he read the page entitled "SATAN AT WORK," and gazed at the pictures of unidentified mammals flattened on various suburban streets. As if it were a gesture he'd rehearsed, Randy straightened his lanky frame, put his hands on his hips, shook his head, and said, "Well, Cowboy, I always knew a quiet guy like you had to have something going on outside the office. Didn't know this was it."

"I clicked the wrong link, that's all."

Jed had gone with Randy for beers after work once. The outing had ended with Jed sneaking out early, while Randy stayed behind to drink his fifth Bud Light and sing along to the jukebox

"Whatever floats your boat, Cowboy," Randy said.

"Randy, I'm serious. I just miss-clicked. I swear," Jed said, his right hand squeezing out an oversized paper clip's symmetry.

"Hey, I'm not the boss man, Cowboy. But if I was, I might switch you to decaf."

Randy was always talking about switching people to decaf. He gave Jed a military salute and walked out of his cube. Watching Randy leave, Jed thought how all this could have been avoided if Scooter had just kept the doll for himself.

The vividness of what he'd witnessed that morning was beginning to fade as Jed drove home. He told himself that whatever had happened, or whatever he thought had happened, would never happen again. There would never be a reason to contact any of the eight carefully researched voodoo experts he'd notated on the yellow legal pad lying on the passenger seat. Still, as he turned the key and opened his apartment door, he prayed silently that he'd find the voodoo doll motionless on his dresser. He also harbored the fear that he'd find the ugly doll had gone berserk in his absence and ransacked the place; that it had carved pentagrams into the walls and learned to speak in tongues.

He swung the door open. Standing on top of his dresser, the doll moved its arms as if stacking things on high shelves. These mundane actions were somehow far more frightening than the aggressive behaviors Jed had feared. The easy movements suggested longevity and permanence. A short burst of illogical animation would surely end quickly, but the figurine could go on like this for days, maybe even months or years. The familiarity was eerie.

Jed snatched the doll. Again, it grew rigid in his grasp. He thought about throwing it against the wall, but was conscious that such a violent reaction would only confirm a slipping mental state. He placed the doll back on the dresser, where it continued to organize its invisible items, placing some things down low and others so high it had to extend to its full twelve-inch height. When finished, the doll breathed deeply, its chest inflating and deflating in what would have sounded like a deep exhalation or sigh. It removed its felt jacket, walked over to the boom box, and hung the garment on the volume knob.

Jed gently placed his wallet and keys in their usual spot

and took a seat at the foot of his bed. The doll sat on Jed's wallet. It extended its right arm for a moment and then leaned back as if supported by a large cushion. It appeared to be watching something, maybe an invisible TV.

The doll's relaxed state put Jed, to some degree, at ease. As the clay head peered into space, Jed took the opportunity to set up his laptop and compose an e-mail to his eight well-researched voodoo experts. The body of the message was the same for each recipient:

> *I'm writing because I know you to be an expert on voodoo mythology and the Vodun religion. I'd like to know if you've ever heard stories of voodoo dolls moving on their own. Are there any rituals aimed at making dolls come to life? I would greatly appreciate any answer you can give me.*
>
> *Sincerely,*
> *Jed Kendall*

Jed chose his words carefully, not wishing to suggest that he actually believed his voodoo doll could move, yet still hoping to invite a retelling of any folklore or anecdote that could shed light on what was happening in his apartment.

This proactive approach left Jed with a sense of accomplishment. He looked at his dresser where the voodoo doll was engaged in some complicated abdominal exercise. The doll lay on its back with its legs bent at a forty-five-degree angle. It reached left arm-end to right leg and right arm-end to left leg in a quick tempo, and Jed wondered why his lunacy was so unlike romantic fictional accounts, which so often included more impressive delusions. Why did his descent into madness involve a mini-figurine intent on keeping a shapely figure?

Following the plan of action he'd set for himself at work, Jed next dug out his old dorm directory and dialed the number for Roy's family in Santa Monica. Mr. Gill didn't seem to remember Jed, or even pretend to. Still, he gave Jed Roy's cell number. Jed tried to rehearse lines in his head before he called: "Roy, so what's the story with this voodoo doll?" or, "Roy, how was New Orleans?" But thinking about the conversation only made Jed more anxious. He wasn't good on the phone. It was usually best just to dial without thinking too much.

"Hello?"

"Hello, Roy. It's Jed. Jed Kendall." Jed could hear the background murmur of a multitude of voices. It sounded like Roy was at a bar or a party.

"No fucking shit! Jed Kendall. How are you?"

Roy's enthusiasm left Jed unsure whether or not he was being made fun of. Self-conscious, Jed became more direct.

"Roy, what is this thing you sent me? Where did you get it?"

"You like it, huh? Scooter's got all sorts of tricks up his sleeve."

Maybe Roy was drunk. Freshmen year Roy had been

drunk quite a few times. "But, I mean, where did you get it, Roy?"

"This friend of mine has a buddy in New Orleans, and this guy's cousin is a full-on voodoo priest or some shit. But how are you, man? How's life?"

"Look, I need to know where you got the doll."

"Jesus, Jed. A little tightly wound, aren't you?"

Roy paused. Jed realized now that he'd made it clear he hadn't called just to chat.

Roy started up again in a softer tone. "Yeah, well, this voodoo priest told me to forget all of those phony shops in the French quarter and that I should go to the park bench by the river where you can get the authentic stuff from a Creole bum who sells these dolls like a New York street vendor sells Rolexes. This is the real deal, Jed. No fucking around."

"So do they put spells on it or something?"

"The hell if I know. I just picked the creepiest looking one. Jed, man, how you doing? It sounds like you could stand to loosen up a bit. I'm coming to San Francisco in a couple months. You should drive up."

Jed looked over at his dresser. The figure was now standing with hands on hips twisting its torso, working its obliques.

"I don't know. I'm pretty busy with work." Jed tried to picture himself flying to New Orleans and walking the banks of the Mississippi looking for a bum hawking voo-doo dolls. It didn't seem productive.

"Yeah, I understand."

Jed realized he wasn't getting anywhere. "Look, Roy, I've got to get going."

"That all you called about, Jed? About the doll?"

This was his last chance to come clean to Roy about what had happened, if anything had in fact happened.

"I just wanted to know where you got it."

"Yeah, I thought you'd like that. Hey, thanks for calling, Jed. I'll send you a postcard when I get to San Francisco."

"Okay. Thanks, Roy."

There was nothing left for Jed to do but sit the rest of the night and wait for the doll to stop moving. He certainly couldn't turn his back on the thing, and while he thought about leaving the apartment, he couldn't stand the thought of missing the exact moment the doll stopped moving, and he would be able to say to himself, "See, Jed, nothing to worry about. It's all over."

"Hey, ugly doll," Jed said. "Can you hear me?" The doll didn't react. It continued its exercise routine, rolling its torso in wide circles. Jed knew that specific exercise was good for lower-back pain. "Do you think you're going to stop this soon? Can you give 'ole Jed his sanity back?" The doll didn't react.

If there were anyone he trusted in Bakersfield, he would have had him come over immediately to test if he could see the doll's movements. In Bakersfield, though, he had only colleagues. There was Charlotte, the girl he saw some-times at the stable. He considered her a friend, or "just friends" as Charlotte termed it, but he couldn't simply call her up and invite her to the apartment. He had friends and family in Gilroy, but he wasn't willing to explain this over the phone. Having an on-the-scene witness was the only way to avoid being perceived as insane. The only thing to do was to watch and wait. He ordered a pizza.

By the time the doorbell rang, the voodoo doll had been jumping and gyrating to inaudible music for nearly twenty minutes. Jed opened his apartment door as wide as he could, all but inviting the pizza boy inside in hopes that the skinny teenager might notice the dancing voodoo doll and say, "Hey, what the fuck is that?" Such a statement would confirm Jed's sanity. But the kid simply kept his bloodshot eyes on Jed, and said, "That will be seventeen dollars and seventy-six cents, sir."

Jed took the pizza from the teenager, walked slowly across the room, and placed the box on top of the television. "Let me get my wallet," Jed said. He walked over to his dresser and very conspicuously picked up his leather Wrangler wallet. Jed lingered next to the voodoo doll that was now performing a carefully choreographed dance rou-tine that Jed was certain had been lifted from MTV. The pizza boy didn't notice the doll. Jed watched the teenager run his hand through his hair and gaze at the inside of the apartment as if it were thick with smoke. Meanwhile, the voodoo doll began a highly suggestive series of pelvic thrusts. Only after Jed had offered a twenty did the kid's eyes appear to refocus. "Oh, thank you, sir," he said.

The delivery boy turned slowly and left. Jed analyzed the interaction. Had the teenager been oblivious, high, or did the dancing figure simply not exist? Jed had missed his opportunity for a second opinion. He ran to the door, opened it, and looked into the hallway. The pizza boy stood before the elevator, his skinny shoulders hunched forward.

"Hey," Jed yelled. "Can you come in here a minute? I've really got to show you something."

The teenager turned toward Jed, his mouth open. Finally, he said, "Sorry, man, I don't go that way." The elevator bell chimed and the kid stepped in with a single long stride.

Jed sat on the bed and ate his pizza. The doll had finished dancing and now seemed to be cooking, one arm holding an invisible fry pan and the other hovering above and circling in a stirring motion. If there'd been smells or sounds to accompany the doll's actions, Jed thought he could deduce what it was cooking. Instead, he had to guess, and for some reason decided that the left hand looked to be flipping a spatula so as to suggest an omelet. As he finished the last slice of pizza, Jed's laptop chimed to notify him he'd received an e-mail.

Ordinarily, Jed would have washed the pizza grease off

his hands before touching his government-subsidized computer. Now, he simply wiped up quickly with a dry paper towel to read the reply from one of his voodoo experts. The Tulane professor.

Mr. Kendall,

There is a legend of voodoo dolls so confused by muddled spells that they take on the traits of the very person they were designed to mimic. As the story goes, it is the person who influences the doll in such a case rather than the doll who influences a person's behavior. When this happens, the voodoo doll is called a who doin' doll. Unlike a voodoo doll, a who doin' doll has no potential for spells. It is simply the odd waste product of sloppy voodoo. I hope this helps.

Dr. Shelton

While the professor's response was as close to a clear explanation as Jed had dared hope for, the prospect of buying into an ancient voodoo legend, of giving weight to magical spells, terrified Jed more than accepting what he'd seen as a grand illusion. The idea that some bum in New Orleans had somehow hexed his Bakersfield existence was unacceptable. What was perhaps most frightening was that this small figure was a window into someone else's life. Sweating now, Jed wiped his hands with a fresh paper towel. He typed a response in the hope of reaching the professor before he left his computer.

*Who makes the doll do this? Who will the doll mimic?
When will it stop moving?*

Jed

Jed sent it off and waited for a response. The second hand ticks of his Wal-Mart clock seemed to echo in his apartment during his three-minute wait. The professor replied:

It's just mythology, but I suppose the doll could be mimicking anybody at all, just as a voodoo doll can represent anyone.

How did you get my e-mail address?

If Jed could have dragged the professor through his computer and into his apartment, Dr. Shelton would have seen the voodoo doll eating its dinner, slicing into its tasty dish, and occasionally dabbing its widespread grin in a way to suggest that it used a cloth napkin far more sophisticated than Jed's length of paper towel.

"Are you mocking a real person, doll?" The figurine ignored him again, and this time Jed wondered if it was because whoever had crafted the doll had forgotten to give it ears.

The professor's note was no comfort. Instead, it brought into Jed's mind a whole realm of possibilities he'd never considered. He was now forced to speculate. Who was at home right now, eating dinner and lifting his fork to his mouth in time with the hideous doll? How many more nights would Jed come home and spend time analyzing the doll's routine in search of clues as to its true identity? The clerk at the drugstore would have to be scrutinized for mannerisms similar to the doll's, as would the gas station attendant, the waitress at the Midnight Diner, and everyone else. The nine hours he'd spent fretting over his doll's sudden animation would be nothing compared to the ongoing torture of knowing he was watching someone real through the figurine's actions.

Jed watched the doll scrubbing dishes. He realized there would never be an easy way to unravel the mystery of his who doin' doll. Deducing any explanation for who had hexed the doll, why, and whom it represented would take years of research and treks through Louisiana, Haiti, and Africa. Or, he could drive himself crazy searching each continent for the object of his doll's mimicry. The remainder of his life would turn into a hopeless search across the globe.

The figurine stopped its dishwashing and became inanimate again when Jed wrapped his fist around a delicate twig leg. Jed closed it inside an old shoebox and placed the box deep inside his bedroom closet. His apartment now looked like it did before. Safe. Simple. Regular. But were things back to normal? Jed couldn't help but wonder if the shoebox shuddered with life. He'd removed the problem, but hadn't solved it. Jed watched his closet door, half expecting to see it swing open with an eerie creak and the little clay head to peak out. After just a few minutes, Jed fished the box out and opened it. There was his doll, on hands and knees, one hand moving in a circular motion as if cleaning a spill.

He could have thrown the doll into the alley dumpster and sent it away with the morning trash, but, like the shoebox, that would not have satisfied him. These solutions provided no finality. Jed knew he'd forever imagine the doll miming out mopping while standing on top of the municipal landfill, or slicing bread amidst acres of Hefty bags. Jed needed to witness the doll stop. He placed it back on his bureau.

Jed woke the next morning to the buzz of his alarm clock, sat up in his futon bed, and looked toward his doll. It was already awake and moving, running its left hand through its wiry hair in long strokes. Jed realized he'd never really looked closely at the doll's actions but had simply been fixated on the implausible fact that it had moved at all. Now he could see the doll was brushing its long hair. The figurine then leaned forward and circled its double row of straight white teeth with the end of its arm. Though Jed was unfamiliar with the female morning bathroom routine, and his doll did not have lips, he could see it was applying lipstick. It was clearly a woman. Jed suddenly felt a bit guilty, and excited, about catching a glimpse into the doll's most intimate behavior. He thought about looking away as the doll continued to examine her face in an invisible mirror, then remembered that her hollow black eyes had never before seemed to recognize his existence. Still leaning forward a bit, the doll fluffed her wispy hairs with her stump hands and turned her head slightly, perhaps to inspect blemishes on her nose or cheek. Jed thought of the doll for the first time as a person with a human face.

Every weekday morning, Jed woke at 6 a.m., ate dry toast, drank coffee and orange juice by 6:15 a.m., then into the shower, all in time for an 8 a.m. arrival at his government cube. However, on this day he'd spent a good fifteen minutes sitting in bed watching the doll get ready for her day. Jed then skipped breakfast, and once he got into the shower, stayed too long. While the warm water washed over him, Jed began piecing together a complete personality from the doll's cumulative actions. She liked to dance, exercise, clean, cook, smoke an occasional cigarette, and lived alone. In the morning, she spent a good deal of time in front of the mirror, and her careful inspection of her face made Jed believe it was possible she was a bit self-conscious. Jed had heard it said that beauty lies within, but in his doll's case, he believed beauty lay in some young woman's apartment miles away from Bakersfield.

Freshman year Roy had dated Karen for nearly six months. She had spent a good deal of time in their room, but Jed rarely talked to her when she was there. Karen had always filled the space with the smell of her perfume and shampoos and often wore tight-fitting sweaters that looked soft to the touch. Each time Jed had seen her, her long blonde hair had looked as though just brushed to a golden sheen. Jed had rarely looked her in the eye because he'd been certain that if he had, both she and Roy would have instantaneously known that he wanted to touch her smooth hair and rest his cheek against her soft sweater.

Jed had probably spent more time around Karen than he had with any other girl his own age. For that reason, while Jed worked in his government cube that day, he couldn't help but compare his hideous voodoo doll to Roy's ex-girlfriend. Jed imagined there were similarities between what he had seen his doll doing and the things Karen might have done in her everyday life. And while Jed did not condone smoking, or understand what joy could be gleaned from choreographed dance, he began to think his doll could be mimicking someone whom he might well like to know. Jed decided it might be tolerable, perhaps even enlightening, to have her around his apartment for a while. And, since she was going to be with him all of the time, it was only fitting he give her a name.

Sitting in the safety of his cubicle, Jed turned to a new page of his legal pad, took out a ballpoint pen, and made a list. Karen? Already taken. Kelly, Kristen, Kristy? Jed moved toward a more systematic approach. Ann, Anna, Annabelle, Anita, Barbara, Betsy—before too long he had filled several pages. He lifted the pad off his desk and held it at eye level to read it over.

"Is that the Cowboy's black book?"

Jed swiveled to face the direction of the voice. Randy loomed, hands on slim hips, coffee breath wafting toward Jed's nose.

"Oh, hey, Randy. These are just—"

"They're just the names of your Saturday-night honeys? Is that it, Cowboy?"

Randy smiled and Jed could see that the gum line between his wide-spaced teeth was discolored slightly, brown.

"I may get a pet," Jed said.

"I bet you will, Cowboy. A sweet kitty, or a wild beast? Raarrrr!" Randy made claws with his fingertips and gave a soundless chuckle. His chest and shoulders bobbed, and he curled his upper lip. Before Jed could figure out why his lie had failed, Randy saluted and left the cube.

Jed looked at his pad and circled the name Olympia. It was the only one on the list whose beauty, Jed felt, could override the ugliness of the refuse-constructed doll. Olympia sounded important, symbolic of something, and Jed thought this unimaginable happenstance was probably representative of something greater for both him and Olympia. Something grandiose was happening, and Olympia seemed the name for it.

Growing up, Jed's family had owned a golden retriever named Mac, and each day Jed rode home on the school bus, he'd picture what it would be like to be reunited with his dog. While sitting on his vinyl seat, Jed could imagine opening the front door and seeing Mac running toward him with his tongue out and his tail wagging. Now, driving his truck back from the Wild Horse and Burro Division, Jed found himself imagining stepping through the front door of his apartment to see Olympia atop his bureau. She might be on the phone, or completing household chores, but she would doubtlessly be there to greet him.

Jed opened the door. Olympia sat on the dresser, peering into her lap. She moved an arm-end from one knee to the other, then again, which made Jed think she was reading a book or magazine. Jed placed his wallet next to her, knowing sometimes Olympia liked to sit on it. Her upright position atop the wallet looked much more comfortable than her current pose. Jed sat on his bed and watched her read. He tried to imagine her bristly hair as a long, straight blonde mane. Though her mouth still appeared a skull-like row of teeth, Jed knew her lips had been carefully coated with a glossy sheen that morning.

Jed looked at his watch and realized it was six-thirty. Even inside his apartment, he could feel the late-September desert sun give way to cool dusk. He'd been watching Olympia read for nearly a half-hour. He got up to boil water for a pasta dinner, but stopped on the way to the stove and contemplated Olympia's positioning. Jed was uncertain of her relationship with the objects in his room. She seemed able to utilize his wallet as a lounge chair and the boom box as a coat hook, yet also maintained a relationship with elsewhere-existing objects. She held invisible items, cooked on a stove Jed couldn't see, and peered into her own TV. She clearly had some concept of Jed's apartment space: she never fell off the dresser, yet didn't climb down to explore either. It occurred to Jed that Olympia might be more comfortable if he were to provide her with a few small pieces of furniture.

Jed pulled an empty Cheerios box out of the trash, pulled his army knife from his pocket, and fetched some masking tape. He built a cardboard chair and placed it on the dresser. Jed pressed on the seat to test its durability. Next, using the same cardboard box, Jed made a table. He cut rectangles out of an old fleece blanket and laid them atop one another, making a bed. He sat again, admiring the habitat he'd created. Olympia still read on the dresser top. Jed thought about taking over a small dish of water to serve as a bathtub, but thought it might be inappropriate to encourage Olympia to bathe in front of him. He would no longer feel comfortable watching her remove her gemstone jacket and tattered pants. He liked to think of it as her white picket fence, though he did admit to himself that it looked more like a corral.

When Olympia walked over to her Cheerios chair an hour later and sat down, Jed felt like a barrier between them had fallen. Their separate existences overlapped. A plate of half-eaten pasta in his lap, Jed asked, "Do you like it, Olympia?" He was instantaneously embarrassed by his irrational exuberance, the too-wide grin on his face, then relaxed a bit when he remembered the doll didn't have any ears and that her eyes were cavernous black holes with no capacity for sight. "Do you like it? I made it myself," he said. "Handcrafted from a single piece of lumber." She tossed her hair with her arm-end, then reached out as if pointing a remote control. She nestled her clay head into the chair's headrest. Jed stood, extended his pointed finger, and gently stroked Olympia's bumpy, twig knee. She didn't turn rigid as she had before, but reclined in her chair. Jed wondered if the real Olympia, the human version, might also be feeling his light touch. He continued to run his fingertip along her leg, fearing at any moment the spell would be broken and the doll would return to its stiff state. "Olympia, do you think you might speak to me someday? You do have a mouth," Jed said. The doll's vacant eyes stared off toward the unseen television screen.

Olympia slept on her fleece-lined bed when Jed woke the next morning. She lay on her side, knees pulled up to her stomach, her chest moving in and out with the slow breathing of deep sleep. "Good morning, my pet," Jed said. It was his first attempt at creating a term of endearment for his female companion, but even to his own ear it fell flat. It sounded overly Victorian, so Jed thought he would try a nickname more in line with his ranch-hand roots like "little doggie" or "fine filly." Jed placed his hand close to Olympia's face to see if he could feel her breath, but although her body moved during her inhales and exhales, she wasn't taking in or expelling air. Jed told himself that in a few days that could change, just as her relationship with his furnishings and his touch had.

Though Jed had created a comfortable environment for Olympia, it occurred to him that it was silly to confine her to his dresser top. There was no reason why she shouldn't accompany him to work. Of course he wouldn't leave her on his desktop for Randy and others to see. He could easily create a space for her inside one of his file cabinet drawers. The tall drawer walls would create an atmosphere similar to a New York City loft, complete with exposed beams. Jed packed Olympia and her furniture into a shoebox.

He left the file drawer under his desk open just a crack, in case Olympia preferred a bit of light. The opening also allowed Jed to see Olympia sitting on her Cheerios-box throne, arms raised in front of her as if she were also working at a desk. Like Jed, Olympia apparently held an office job.

Occasionally she moved from her seat and walked around. Jed guessed she was probably strolling to the printer, or perhaps over to the water cooler. Watching

Olympia during the day cut into Jed's productivity, but he could think of no clear policy against what he was doing. The handbook said no pets at work, no children, but Olympia didn't fall into either category. At the end of his day, and, by the look of her posture, near the end of Olympia's, Jed packed the doll into his shoebox and headed home. He put the box on the passenger seat. "Long day at the office, ay, little filly?" It sounded right. They headed home along the wide, hot streets of downtown Bakersfield.

Packing Olympia up before leaving for work in the morning became part of Jed's routine. He built in five extra minutes for the task and now woke at 5:55 a.m. On the weekend too he put Olympia on the front seat of the pickup when driving to the grocery store or to the stable. He got to know her routines, her body language, her hobbies and habits. She was a lot like him: a homebody for the most part, a hard worker, a reader, and a movie buff, though on the weekends she often drank too much which impaired her walking. She smoked the occasional cigarette and gab- bed on the phone a lot. Jed knew she was beautiful. She took great pains in her appearance both before bed and in the morning. She ate reasonable portions, worked out quite a bit, and liked to dance. She chose her clothes carefully, sometimes dressing more than once to get her outfit right (although to Jed she always appeared to put on the same gemstone jacket and torn pants). And because he knew she was beautiful, Jed was not surprised when her habits started to change, when it became clear she'd found a boyfriend.

Jed first started to recognize certain meals as dinner dates based on Olympia's posture, careful use of invisible utensils, and head movements that implied mid-meal conversation. Walks to her doorstep, which to Jed looked like laps around his dresser top, ended at first with hugs, then more recently kissing. Jed noticed she talked differently on the phone, standing up during some calls rather than slumped in her usual seated position. When this happened, Jed presumed Olympia had her boyfriend on the line. Jed knew Olympia was lonely, like him. He was glad she'd found a companion and even thought briefly that perhaps this meant he would also find love. He said as much to Olympia one night while falling to sleep. "Maybe I'll find someone too, Olympia. Then we'll both have someone else, someone we can actually talk with." The lights off, Jed could still make out Olympia's small body in silhouette, the street lamps' light coming through his window. She lay curled up and asleep, breathing heavily.

A few days later, Jed woke during the middle of the night to the sound of Olympia flopping down on the dresser. He turned on his light and saw that her chair had been overturned. Olympia lay flat on her back. At first Jed thought an invisible assailant was attacking her. He popped out of bed wanting to grab hold of her and return her to her frozen state. Then Jed noticed her arms were outstretched and bent just slightly, her neck stretched up, and her head was tilted to one side. Olympia was in an embrace. Her legs opened up and then wrapped around an invisible body. She looked clumsy. Jed hoped she was at least drunk, but it was Wednesday and Olympia never drank during the week. A moment later, Olympia sat upright, grabbed her waistband, and shimmied out of her ratty orange pants. She removed her jacket. With her string-bound twig and wire limbs exposed, Olympia lay flat on her back. Her hips gyrated slowly, her head tilted back. Her clay head scraped against the dresser top in time with her body's rhythmic motion. Though disgusted, Jed could not look away. Olympia's movements became more emphatic, until it was over and she lay still. Not moving from her spot on the bare dresser, she curled up and slept. Jed stayed awake longer, explaining away her actions. He felt like he'd witnessed his childhood sweetheart defiled. It didn't seem like Olympia to act so rashly, but she was lonely and impressionable. Given the chance, Jed might have done the same thing on a Wednesday night.

The first act had been jarring, yet forgivable. After the second, third, and fourth occurrences it grew tiresome. Afterwards, Olympia's lifestyle became repugnant to Jed. He often closed her inside her shoebox to keep from witnessing her numerous sex acts. Her positioning became more creative, and it seemed to Jed that her jacket and pants spent as much time at the bottom of the shoebox or on top of his dresser as they did on her thin body. It wasn't just before and after the workday either. Once during his lunch hour Jed peered into his file drawer and saw Olympia naked, bent over her Cheerios chair in an almost impossible position. Not only did Jed find it sickening, but he also wondered if perhaps this pose might affect the integrity of her twig construction. A leg might simply splinter and snap off. It looked unhealthy, yet she didn't ease up.

Perhaps Olympia was not like Jed at all, but more like Roy. Jed had unwillingly heard tales of Roy's sexual exploits and had always wondered about the type of young woman to be involved in the grotesque tales. Perhaps it had been a woman like Olympia, a sex-fiend, MTV-watching smoker who bar hopped on weekends until she couldn't walk straight. Olympia didn't even appear anymore to take the same care in her appearance. Workdays sometimes ended before five o'clock. Her dancing had become a bit too seductive, almost embarrassing and lewd. The doll went through her exercise routine far less frequently. Coupled with more meals out, Jed was sure she was gaining weight.

Jed was as unproductive without Olympia under his desk as he had been with her there. At every moment, he couldn't help but think about what she was doing. He wondered whether she was meeting her boyfriend for a noontime quickie, or chatting with him secretly over her workplace phone while twirling the cord around her free hand. Jed could foresee no easy solution to his relationship with Olympia. He couldn't very well get rid of her simply for her crude behavior. She wasn't aware he could see into her bedroom.

Because Jed worked eight to five Monday through Friday, he had never considered that a voodoo priestess might enjoy a more nebulous workweek. To Jed, an "expert" was someone who checked her e-mail daily, if not hourly. In Jed's mind, experts gave answers quickly and got their facts straight. He had all but forgotten about the experts other than Dr. Shelton, whom he'd e-mailed weeks earlier, until he recognized an address, widowparis@st-louis1.net, as belonging to a voodoo priestess. She had her own website. Jed had counted this against her during his initial research. He thought it unlikely that she was authentic, but at the time had been desperate for any information. The message read:

> *Monsieur Jed,*
>
> *Only a doll with the serpent spirit inside can move that way. A doll like that is too strong; a dangerous type of witching has been done. You got to stop that doll. Cover it with mud from the Mississippi. That'll keep the spirit from seeing the human world, and he'll leave the doll. I can send you mud. $50 a jar. Cash.*
>
> *- ⊕⊕⊕*

It sounded like the moneymaking scheme of a web-based voodoo guru, but there was no doubt Olympia's allure was powerful, and Jed considered it possible he'd been bewitched in some way. He certainly wasn't himself.

The end of daylight saving time had stolen an hour from the night, and Jed drove home around 5:15 p.m. under a black sky. The desert chill set in earlier too, and Jed wore his sheepskin jacket over his dress shirt. He stopped at an ATM and withdrew fifty dollars. He hadn't decided the priestess was right, but hers was a proposition worth considering.

Jed stood outside his apartment, his key still in the door's lock, and already could hear the rhythmic bumping of Olympia against his dresser top. Jed walked in and saw her naked, quivering legs in the air, back arched so that only her shoulders and ass touched the dresser's surface. He grabbed a T-shirt from a dresser drawer and threw it over her. He could tell from the relief imprint of her body that she'd resorted to her lifeless state. Her legs had relaxed, and lay flat. Jed picked her up inside the shirt, like he would a dead rodent, and placed her in the shoebox. But Olympia was insatiable that day, and Jed heard the same noises again just an hour later. It happened for a third time that night.

The Olympia Jed had constructed in his mind, the beautiful, lonely young woman in need of furniture and friendship, had vanished. Jed wondered now if in fact

Olympia was with just one man or whether her sexual appetite could only be quenched by several partners. Really, nothing about her appealed to Jed any longer. He felt as though he were stuck in a movie theater for weeks watching an abhorrent, unsympathetic character on screen.

He reached into his pocket and fingered his Swiss army knife. The blade was likely too short, but a kitchen knife could easily sever Olympia's clay head from her limber body. Her stick limbs could be chopped into an unrecognizable mishmash. A grocery bag could serve as a graveyard. Dr. Shelton had assured him, "A who doin' doll has no potential for spells." Destroying the doll would be harmless to the human Olympia. She could go on scrumping day in and out, and in and out. The more he thought about it, the more it seemed the only rational thing to do. Forget the Mississippi mud, forget tracking the doll's object of mimicry, Jed wanted a return to normalcy, a clean break.

Jaw clenched, Jed did his best to suggest a nonchalant air as he walked into the kitchen nook. As he reached into a drawer and withdrew his sharpest carving knife, he feared the doll might suddenly develop the cognitive capacity necessary to foresee her demise. Jed walked back to his dresser with the knife behind his back, like a horror-movie stalker. He reached out and grabbed the doll. Although asleep, she grew rigid, and Jed used his left hand to press Olympia's ugly face into the dresser's wooden surface. With his right hand, he held the knife an inch above her twig neck and chopped her head from her folk-art body with a single violent strike. Olympia's lumpy skull scooted loudly across the bureau.

Next, Jed went to work on the limbs, slicing right through her bright orange pants. He cut across her thin waistline, through her arms, and just in case the doll possessed some sort of voodoo spirit, cut into the spot where her heart would be, comforted to find only more twigs and wire.

Soon there was nothing left resembling a human form, only bits of twig and cloth. Olympia was gone. Jed breathed heavily and stared at the mess on top of his gashed dresser. The apartment was still and lifeless, and Jed felt a calm creeping back into him. All that was left was easily cleaned with a broom and dustpan. As Jed swept up the pieces and secured them in a plastic grocery bag, he thought of the wonderful predictability of arriving at work tomorrow with no dancing doll left behind in his apartment.

Roy called late in the afternoon that Saturday.

"Yo, Jed. I'm in San Fran."

"Yeah, you at a conference?" Jed hadn't spoken to anyone outside of work since chopping up Olympia and was thankful for the call.

"Yep. How you doing, Jed? How's work? How are the wild ponies?"

"Okay, okay. Keeping me busy, you know."

"How about the little fillies? Heh?"

Jed felt obliged to chuckle, but the question pained him. "Their numbers are down a bit this year, Roy."

"I hear you, man. I hear you. Listen, come meet me. I'm downtown in the Grand Hyatt. The company set me up pretty nice."

Jed looked toward his bureau. The spot where the doll had once lived was marred. The evidence of his violence made Jed want to leave the room, maybe even leave Bakersfield. It had all been so gruesome and ridiculous.

"Yeah, Roy, I'll come up."

"Yeah, we'll see the city a bit. Gotta help me get through this per diem."

Jed got off the phone and packed an overnight bag. He did his best to dress for a night out in the city, which meant office attire: a blue dress shirt, black pants, and leather shoes. He looked in the mirror, ran his hand over his flattop's stiff spikes, and wondered if he should grow his hair out. In his sock drawer, Jed kept a bottle of Stetson, a gift from his dad that he had used sparingly since the age of sixteen. He dabbed a bit behind his ear. Reaching the door, he turned and looked back, a quick check to make sure everything was in order before he left for the day. On the dresser, almost hidden by his stereo, he noticed one of Olympia's purple buttons sparkling in the light of his Wal-Mart lamp. He closed the door, got into his pickup, and headed north.

LURKING

You hear a bang, and your eyes snap open. You were asleep and need a moment to figure out whether or not you heard the noise in a dream. Before you come to any firm realization, your wife gasps, a loud inhalation, and jolts upright. Seeing her, you realize you're awake, you remember you're married, and that your infant son is sleeping in the bassinet beside the bed.

Your wife sits up and turns toward you, eyes unusually wide, hair matted.

"Did you hear that?" she says.

"Yeah," you say.

"What was it?"

"I think it came from the living room, or maybe the kitchen." You visualize the rooms in your apartment and think of items on high shelves and dishes you may have haphazardly stacked.

"Is the front door locked?"

"Yes."

"Are you sure?"

"Yes."

She stares past you, toward the bedroom door.

"What if someone is out there?" she says.

"Nobody is out there."

"Well, what made that noise?"

"Something fell."

She pushes herself upright, as if doing so will allow her to see into the next room.

"Do you want me to check it out?"

She turns toward you and smiles sheepishly. "Yes."

Because you know she's proud, you make a joke: "You want me to get beat up first?"

"Yes. If I hear you scream, I'll run out and save you." She pushes you out of bed with her cold, bare feet. "Go, go."

You smile at her.

As a child, you'd feared that snakes hid under your bed and that they would strike your ankles as you stepped onto the floor. You walk away from the bed quickly and move through the bedroom door. You know there is nothing in the living room, but it's dark and you're still somewhat afraid of the dark. It is where villains hide, fictional and real. Dark alleys, dark corners, and dark living rooms should be avoided. Your heart beats quickly, which you find embarrassing. Thank goodness nobody knows.

No one could have gotten into the apartment. You're going through the motions to comfort your wife, yet you can't help but imagine what you would do if confronted by a bloodthirsty brute. You make a fist with your right hand. You feel tendons and muscles awaken inside your forearm. You could hit someone hard if you really had to, if it came down to it.

You decide against turning the lights on, thinking darkness will be an advantage in a scuffle. You move slowly into the center of the living room and are relieved not to see anyone. Then you imagine someone hiding, waiting to leap out. You look under your desk, behind the television, and under the dining table. You turn around suddenly, thinking that the space between the couch and the bookshelf could provide a shadowy refuge for a crouching assailant. You walk over slowly. You imagine seeing the dim outline of a figure as you move closer, and you squeeze your fist tighter with each step. You arrive at the shadowy hideout. Nothing. Nothing in the kitchen. Nothing anywhere. You start looking for a broken plate, for a fallen picture frame, but you don't see anything. "I don't see anything," you say. It's not loud enough for your wife to hear. Talking loudly would wake the baby. You're making this statement for yourself. Making statements aloud can help convince you of their validity. You've done this before. You remember practicing, "My fiancé and I…" then, "My wife and I …" then, "My son …" After a while, the phrases felt right.

Again you say, "I don't see anything." You try to calm your frenzied heartbeat. You try to relax your clenched right fist and stop thinking of it as a weapon.

You walk back toward the bedroom feeling guilty about your pace. There could still be something lurking in the shadows. You didn't find any telltale shards of ceramic or glass. You didn't look that carefully, but you don't want to be out there alone anymore either. As you come through the door, your wife smiles at you.

"Find anything?" she says.

"No. Something fell. We'll find it in the morning."

"No robbers?"

"No robbers."

"Thanks for checking it out."

"No problem," you say. You stand next to the bed, bend down, and kiss her on the forehead. "You're lucky to have a strong, studly man looking out for you." Your wife pushes you again with her cold feet.

You walk to your side of the bed and get in with a small hop. You stroke your wife's thick, curly hair, and you start to feel better. Your heartbeat slows. There never was anything out there. There never could have been. Your wife lies back down, and you watch her close her eyes.

You pull the quilt up toward your chin as if it were armor. You watch the knob of the bedroom door and imagine what you would do if it turned. You have an iron, dog-shaped bookend on your nightstand that could bash in somebody's skull. You could get to it quickly.

Your wife falls back to sleep. Her breathing becomes deep and audible. The baby stirs. You hear him sigh and shift. He is also asleep.

You're still awake, and you split your time between staring at the doorknob and glancing at the digital clock on your nightstand. 2:42, 2:48, 2:57, 3:06. Your alarm will go off in less than three hours if the baby doesn't wake you first. You need sleep. No one is out there. You are sure of it. You close your eyes but tell yourself you will keep listening just in case. If someone were to open the door, you would hear it. You would leap up and grab that bookend.

But your body is getting heavy, relaxed. You never hear the creak of the door when you're asleep. You wouldn't know of an intruder until after he'd entered. He could dash into the room, pounce onto the bed, knife in hand, and slit your wife's throat. He could creep slowly toward the bas-sinet with a pillow and quietly suffocate your son. There would be nothing you could do. You'd only be able to say that you had thought the sound had been a falling plate or picture frame. You'd gone out to check, but didn't see anything. You had thought everything was okay.

THE CANARY IN THE COAL MINE

Tradition seeped from every corner of our home, hid beneath the old newspapers on the floor, and hung like a haze in the air. Before reaching working age, I'd lost my father and two brothers to the mines. Mother wore her widowhood and the deaths of her children like a badge of honor. In her mind, they died serving a higher purpose. Blue-collar aristocracy. "You've got a lot to be proud of, Cecil," she'd say. "Your family has saved many miners."

Mother replaced dead loved ones with stories of their heroics. Great-grandfather died just moments before the explosion of '22. Grandfather collapsed of carbon inhalation in the bowels of West Virginia's deepest mine. His death led to the evacuation of thirty workers. Mother assumed I'd work the mines too. In my family, it takes dying to accomplishing anything.

When Mr. Jones placed his extended finger in front of my perch, signaling a first-time request for service, I thought of how I'd witnessed my father and brothers receive the same invitation. I moved only with the urging of my family. My sister and uncle sung words of encouragement. Mother chimed in, her voice wavering, on the verge of proud tears. "Cecil, it's your time, honey," she said. "Go with Mr. Jones." The force of history pushed me onto his pale finger. "Your turn to work today, little one," said Mr.

Jones as he latched the cage door. Without choice, I'd become a coal mine canary.

A miner the others called "Smitty" carried my small cage. My perch swayed with his stride as we proceeded among the miners and donkeys. Tools clanked and jangled on belt loops and in wagons. Everything was of the same coal-colored hue. I pictured my yellow coat shining like a beacon, a flash of color against a humdrum backdrop. Listening to the gab of the miners and rhythmic clop of the donkeys' hooves, I felt, for the first time, a touch of pride. I sang. My own melody mixed well with the sounds of our trudging brigade. As we walked, I thought maybe following in the footsteps of my father held some merit. I thrust my chest out, pushed my beak high, and sang louder.

When we left the sun, everything changed. I stopped singing. The miners hardly talked. The tunnel narrowed and the mountain squeezed us, choking the light and air. Flickering lanterns showed hard rock. I forgot about pride and hoped for resilience, for perseverance. I'd entered the grave of my ancestors. We continued downward, and the temperature dropped. In the darkness, I saw clearly the idiocy of my heritage. Those that had come before had failed to make another choice. Like me, they'd walked like lemmings onto Mr. Jones' inviting finger.

After what must have been a half-mile descent, Smitty placed my cage on the ground. He bent down and looked closely at me through the bars. "You take care of us, you hear?" Smitty's voice was austere. I wanted to say something profound about the commonality of our fear. I only chirped, a strained exclamation denoting nothing in particular.

The miners' broad, sweaty backs moved rhythmically as they swung their picks at the coalface. Steel clanked with each strike, and the walls resonated, threatening collapse. Rock fell away, and new crevices appeared. The scene flickered beneath the lanterns' jumping light. It seemed as if the men were beating a living creature, and I waited for the retaliatory strike—a seepage of deadly gas or a rumbling of falling rock. I imagined gas had already leaked. With every breath, I tasted the air. Would I be able to tell if I was dying, or would death come too fast?

My anxiety grew. The miners had their battle with rock and fatigue, tasks to take their minds off imminent death. I had no such distractions. The walls seemed to close in on me. The ringing of the metal tools became deafening, and the aura of death grew more specific and immediate. I felt lightheaded and nauseous. My breathing quickened. I had to leave. I couldn't wait until the end of our shift.

They turned toward me every now and again, just often enough to make sure I was alive. I held some hope that my expression of horror would somehow transcend the boundaries of our species; that they would take one look at me, sweep me up, and carry me out of the mountain. But each time they glanced in my direction, they turned away without noticing my terror. There was only one way to leave the mine before the end of a shift. I closed my eyes, relaxed my clasp on the perch, and allowed my body to crash to the cage's bottom. Obligation to duty and my commitment to the miners tumbled with me to the cold, iron surface. I lay motionless. Moments later I heard Smitty: "Fellas, the bird! The bird is down!"

Smitty lifted my cage, and soon I swayed again with the scurrying steps of his retreat. I remained still, my eyes closed, and listened to the miners' boots on the tunnel floor and to the jingling of the tools and buckets being lugged up. Their hysteria was my euphoria. I'd altered my destiny. Soon, I felt the warmth of the sun. Recognizing the brightness through my closed eyes, I knew we were safe. I'd survived.

I lay still, contemplating the most delicate and tactful way to come back to life. Around me, I could hear a lot of men, one being Mr. Jones, and they all talked about my death.

"There's something nasty down there, for sure," said Mr. Jones.

I slowly opened my eyes, but remained motionless. My cage, still held by Smitty, was at thigh-height of about a dozen men. Nothing else to do, I raised myself to my feet.

I heard Smitty's voice booming from above the cage. "Jones! Mr. Jones!" he said. "The damn bird is alive!"

My cowardice on display, the miners turned toward me.

For a brief moment, I wished I were still down below. Mr. Jones bent to look at me. "I'll be damned, Smitty. Maybe your bird here was just nappin'. The mine must be all right."

Dozens of dirty faces stared into my cage.

"This one's a faulty alarm," Mr. Jones said to the group. The miners smiled, joked with one another, and retreated to the mine. Mr. Jones grabbed my cage and lifted me to eye level. He breathed audibly. He smelled of coffee. "You cost me a fair bit of money today, bird," he said. I didn't care about Jones' money. I thought of him now as the ringmaster of my family's daily game of Russian roulette. My cage swung with the cadence of his gait as we headed toward his office.

Though no one came out and said it, my fainting spell disgraced the others. I wanted to explain; I wanted to shout, "Don't you see? We have to change. We have to turn away!" But they'd never understand. Any attempt at dialogue would only force them to express their resentment.

To make things worse, everyone who came into the office wanted to talk about the incident. Over the next week, I watched men laughing and teasing Mr. Jones, sometimes pointing over at our cage and calling us "yellow-bellied" or "bird-brained." Mr. Jones always ended the ribbing the same way: "Damndest thing. Damndest thing." I'd stand at the bottom of the cage, look out the office window, and try to ignore my mother's hard looks.

Now when Mr. Jones came to pick one of us in the morning, he never chose me. "Not the broken one," he'd say, while reaching in with his hairy hand. This utterance brought scornful looks, yet I couldn't help but feel relieved. At the same time, taking myself out of circulation increased the risk for the rest of my family. Uncle John and my sister Jane were picked more often.

One day, around midafternoon, we saw the foreboding horse-drawn wagon move past the office window. Mr. Jones used the Black Maria to carry mangled bodies out of the mountain and back to unsuspecting wives. We canaries feared the sight of the Black Maria as much as the families of the mine workers. More often than not, dead miners meant one of our own had also fallen.

That evening when the foreman returned to the office, he carried with him an empty cage. Uncle John was gone. My mother broke into a shaky dirge, a slow staccato of notes that Mr. Jones mistook for hunger. He walked over, deposited a scoop of seed, and said, "Sorry, little ones. I almost forgot. It's been a long day." Seeing that pale hand reach again toward our cage reminded me of our tortured existence. Mr. Jones was the most immovable tradition: keeping us alive so that we could systematically die.

Closing the cage door, Mr. Jones retreated to his desk and began shuffling through papers, writing and writing in the customary manner that followed any appearance of the Black Maria. As the sky darkened, Mr. Jones lit a lantern on his desk. Mother continued to sing, longer than usual, and I wondered if her melancholy notes were meant for me. I fluffed my feathers, creating a shield against my guilt.

John was destined to die from the day of his birth. I tried hard to believe it was his fault for not fighting to change our circumstances, but that kind of explanation was abstract. The easier course of logic was that John's death could have been my own. If it weren't for my cowardice, John would be here with the family instead of me.

With a particularly bad accident such as this, it was Mr. Jones' practice to interview all who might have borne witness to the events. In this case, the most telling testimony came the day after Uncle John's death from a young miner by the name of Perry.

Mr. Jones walked into his office followed by Perry, who entered with his head low, holding his hat in his hand. Jones sat behind his desk. I remained at the bottom of the cage, trying as best I could to appear indifferent.

"Cigarette, Mr. Perry?" said Jones, extending the carved box.

"No thank you, sir."

Jones took a pen out of his desk drawer and began to speak while writing on a clean sheet of paper. "Now Perry, I just want you to tell me what happened, what you saw down there. You're not in any trouble here; I just gotta turn in my paperwork for the state is all."

Perry looked down to his lap and the twisted cap in his hands. "I didn't see everything, sir," he said. "Just before it happened."

"Well, tell me what you know, Perry," said Jones. He hadn't lifted his eyes from his notes.

"Well, me and Smith, Paine, Clark, and Jenkins, we were working in the western quadrant when Smitty saw his canary had gone and dropped over. Me and Paine, we said we were getting out before we dropped too, but Smitty and the rest of 'em didn't want to go. Smitty said a couple of weeks ago his bird fell off its perch for no reason at all and made him look real stupid, so he said he was gonna wait a bit and see if his bird woke up."

Jones leaned over his paper and looked at Perry. "Go on. What happened next?"

"Well, Smitty started shaking the cage a bit, started talking to the bird. Me and Jenkins said we were getting out of there. Smitty said he'd be up soon, but me and Jenkins didn't wait. We got on up."

"Smitty, Clark, and Paine stayed?"

"When we got to the mouth, we were just sitting there gabbin', jokin' about Smitty talking to his bird. We figured the rest of them would be up any minute so we didn't worry."

"But they never came up, is that right?"

"Right, sir. They must've waited too long thinking the bird was just fakin'. It must've been some of that bad air down there."

"Thank you, Perry. That'll be all," said Jones, shifting his eyes back to his desk. Perry rose from his chair and left.

Mother started with that slow dirge again and continued with it for weeks. She didn't sing in mourning, but in shame. The story of my uncle's death could never be retold as one of heroism. It could only be repeated in conjunction with the tale of my folly. My mother's feathers began to fall out, littering the cage floor. No one sang stories about our forefathers. My silence and attempts at seclusion didn't help anyone forget what had happened. Our home smelled of guilt, shame, and anger. No one talked about it, but the tension was palpable. My sister started to refuse work, which meant more trips to the mine for my aunt.

My family wanted me to admit my wrongdoing so they could forgive me. They'd never understand that my refusal of duty was intended as a step toward something else. Recognizing the impasse, I knew it was time to leave.

The cage and confines of Mr. Jones' office weren't much of an impediment. Wood and iron are easy enough to escape with the right timing, planning, and diligence. The greater obstacles are those you cannot see, perhaps not even define. As I flew through the cage door and past Mr. Jones, I felt the weight of my mother's stories on my wings. When darting over the desk, the smell of coal made me weak. Seeing the crack in the screen door, the small flap where the wire mesh had come loose, I felt the tug of a repressed sense of loyalty. Still, I made it through the door-way. I followed the coal road away from the mine, a direction we canaries never traveled. I flew past what I assumed to be the miners' dingy houses.

While flying away from the mines' poisons and the infectious complacency of my family, I knew the broad promise of the outside world could prove just as toxic. I continued, ready to start my own legacy, my own traditions, but deep down I knew I was simply fleeing the past. As I distanced myself, excitement gave way to fatigue. I flew slowly. My fierce defiance transformed into a sense of aimlessness. I wondered if there was any system to warn the coal mine canary of what might come next.

MAX'S COLOSSUS PROBOSCIS

Before I begin this story, please try to understand how difficult it would be to live with a hypersensitive sense of smell. The scent of wet dogs a half-mile away, septic tanks littering the neighborhood, flatulence and body odor wafting from all directions—these are a few of the most common complaints I hear from my patients. I've witnessed the anguish this ailment can cause, and for that reason it didn't surprise me when eighteen-year-old Max Peet flew across the country from Lakeview, California, to my Washington, D.C. laboratory seeking my advice. I'm the best olfactory doctor in the U.S.

Lorraine led Max into my office and sat him across from me. It was January, usually my slow time of year, when snowfall and frost bury many offensive odors. Max behaved like a springtime patient. He leaned forward, his elbow on his knee, his chin in his palm, and his hand covering most of his face. The boy's meek mannerisms made me rethink the intimidating formality of the wood-paneled walls, red-pine bookcases, and gold-framed diplomas that constituted my decorating scheme. He hooked a worn Nike around the leg of his chair as if to brace himself against the coming inquisition.

I spoke the same lines I always do to new patients; it was only Max's half of the conversation that was out of the ordinary.

"Maximillian Peet," I said. No response. "I understand you believe yourself to have an overactive sense of smell."

His face was still pointed downward, but the bob of his head suggested he was nodding in affirmation.

"Well, you've come to the right man, Max. I've treated lots of patients like you. Are you smelling many things right now?"

Again, he nodded, his shiny, overgrown bangs bouncing.

"Max, you may put in your nose plugs. I won't be offended."

It's been my experience that patients with overactive olfactory glands carry a pair of nose plugs to wear when it's socially acceptable. I always invite my patients to use them as a way to demonstrate the depth of my understanding of their condition. It usually impresses them.

"I already have them in," Max said.

Though it was perhaps a bit callous of me, upon hearing Max's answer I became instantly excited about the extent of his ailment. I envisioned a groundbreaking article in the International Journal of Smell Research. I wanted to help the boy of course, but for years I'd been waiting for the ideal patient, one with symptoms so severe he'd react to every olfactory test in my barrage of patented procedures. While you may be appalled to read of my ambition in the face of Max's agony, you must realize every physician at the top of his field, perhaps even your own doctor, is waiting for a case like Max. Deformities are opportunities.

I pulled my tape recorder out of my top desk drawer, pressed the record button, and said, "Max, why don't you tell me when you first felt there might be something abnormal about your sense of smell?"

Max lifted his chin and gave me a hard stare. I have no doubt this gesture was meant as an expression of discontent, but his look also provided me with a glance at the enflamed cartilage of his nasal septum. The size of his nose clearly qualified him as disfigured rather than simply unfortunately proportioned. On the tip of his nose, I noticed a small pimple, and its appearance reminded me of the boy's fragility. Inside Max's nostrils, I saw what looked like custom-made, skin-toned plastic plugs connected with a U-shaped bar. He jolted me out of my trance when he said, "I don't want to speak into the tape recorder. I'm not a lab rat." Max squirmed in his seat, as if awaiting the backlash of his defiance.

I was humbled by the severity of Max's case, as well as anxious about his delicate emotional state. For the first time in years, I wondered if I was in over my head. Self-doubt swept through me in the form of nausea. The acid from my morning coffee swirled in my stomach. Dreams of leading-edge research papers gave way to concerns about simply conducting a proper doctor-patient interview. I'd have to continue delicately.

I pressed the stop button on my recorder. While the absence of an audio tape was detrimental to science, it does save you from the curt and often foul language that would be revealed through transcription. Instead of giving you Max's word-by-word retelling, below are the facts I've gathered from many interviews with the boy and his parents. The truth came to me slowly, piece by piece, and I have set it down here as accurately as I am able.

Max's story begins in the summer of his eighteenth year, a time when he considered himself geographically, psychologically, and chronologically caught in limbo between a humdrum high school existence and college life at UC Santa Cruz. He was sure college would change everything he didn't like about himself. While waiting out the summer, he made and saved money by working thirty hours a week at Baskin-Robbins. There was also a girl-friend in the picture, more of an officially titled individual rather than someone with whom Max spent a great deal of time. She'd spent most of the summer traveling. So his best friend, Dwight, accompanied Max to such attractive locations as the Omniplex, Taco Bell, Tower Records, and the Video Game Venue. Painfully plain, I know. But the boy's uneventful existence was soon interrupted by his bur-geoning sense of smell.

It happened almost instantaneously. One day, while manning the ice cream parlor, Max realized he could clearly smell each flavor of ice cream. Without consulting the "Map of Flavors" by the cash register, Max led himself to the freezer containing the vat of vanilla bean, not for a minute confusing the distinct scent with that of the vanilla chip. Without searching for bits of marshmallow, Max could differentiate rocky road from double chocolate fudge. When the afternoon sun drove masses of cranky customers into the shop, Max gracefully wielded his ice cream scoop like a dessert magician. I'm fairly certain this was the first time he was good at anything.

Just a few days later, Max discovered the downside of possessing such a Herculean nose. When the store trash cans were filled to the rim, he'd catch from across the room the odor of rotting dairy. His nose alerted him when the milk-murky water in the scoop bucket needed changing. The smell of the mildew in-between the floor tiles made him realize his halfhearted mopping had never quite done the job. With the passing of a few more days, he began smelling the salty, sweat-covered customers. The scent of cents drifted into his nostrils each time he opened the cash register—dirty copper, zinc, and nickel coins, as well as paper bills. He detected the stagnant air floating across the counter each time a customer opened the bathroom door.

At first, Max welcomed this experience, even with the malodors. He'd been yearning for something new. "It was like the first time I got high," Max told me. (Although, he later admitted he'd never actually been high.) Heightened aroma awareness was by far the most exciting thing that'd ever happened to him.

Max only became concerned a few days later when he noticed that his nose was also changing on the exterior. What the boy didn't know was that a regional secretion of growth hormone had stimulated the swelling of his olfactory epithelium. It's the same type of chemical secretion that causes gigantism. However, in Max's case, the growth fluid remained in and around his nasal passages. This abnormal growth was not limited to the olfactory epithelium and internal organs; it also infected the skin and cartilage cells in Max's nose. Slowly, Max's nose began to bulge from its normal size to the malformed construction he brought into my office. The tenderness and swelling Max had first noticed was budding growth.

He'd ignored it as long as he could by writing off the soreness as a result of common allergies or perhaps a skin problem. To some degree he'd convinced himself that his acute sense of smell was just another post-puberty body transformation, like sprouting chest hair. Deep down, he knew there was something severely wrong, but it took the big date with Isabel to convince Max that he needed medical attention.

Three days after Isabel's return from Paris, Max picked her up for their first date in more than a month. Something about the jaunt to France made her fancy herself mature, sensual, and sophisticated—characteristics for which Max was not prepared. They went to the Vienna Buffet, and while eating their turkey dinners Isabel told

Max he had the temperament of a Parisian artist. Max was perplexed by her comment, and he could only assume she'd mistaken his silence for deep thought and gentleness.

As a medical professional, I must add that Max's silence at the restaurant could have been his baffled reaction to the cornucopia of smells emitted by the extensive buffet. Even someone with an average sense of smell knows what it's like to walk into a smorgasbord and recognize the scent of mashed potatoes, hot turkey, roast beef, butter rolls, gravy, string beans, and the rest. I can only imagine what this experience was like for Max.

At the conclusion of the meal, Isabel said she was through with "American Hollywood drivel" and suggested they skip the Omniplex and take Max's car to the scenic overlook off Route 22. This is the place in Lakeview where one can actually view the lake, although not at night. After dark the destination becomes more of an excuse than a vista, I'm told.

Driving toward the scenic overlook, Max was as nervous as he was excited about the inevitable groping. After parking the car, he had little time to worry about how best to proceed. As soon as the engine went silent, Isabel began touching and petting Max in ways the boy had previously only fantasized about. She whispered French into his ear and peeled off her clothes. While Max still claims he had previous intimate knowledge of the female body, I believe such an admission to be highly suspect.

The only reason I'm setting this scene is because in order to realize how truly traumatic this experience was for Max, you must have an idea of the difficulty of the situation without any added complications. Max had to contend with all of the emotions associated with one's first sexual experience, plus the burden of his heightened sense of smell. This scene is integral to his case history.

According to Max, the Civic became an airtight lockbox of stench. With Isabel's body close to his, Max could smell all of her ointments and lotions, shampoo, baby powder, perfume, and cinnamon gum. While at first these scents heightened Max's sexual appetite, he then detected less overt but more offensive odors on her body, such as alcohol-based acne medication, chalky makeup, sweat, and depilatory cream. After becoming aware of this second wave of smells, Max no longer envisioned Isabel as his beautiful Aphrodite. Suddenly, she was a sweaty teenager with bad skin. Startled into a new awareness, Max noticed other smells. The scent of the turkey dinner had seeped into their clothing. The sticky pleather of the car seats gave off a strong synthetic odor. Worst, he could smell his own nervousness collecting in the form of sweat on his cotton undershirt. And in the background, a primal scent of sexual arousal grew from their respective loins. Everything was vividly clear and, in turn, outright disgusting. Isabel, oblivious to Max's change in temperament, reached into her purse and pulled out a condom.

According to Max, as soon as he heard the sound of Isabel tearing open the wrapper, he was hit by the medicinal smells of latex, spermicidal lubricant, and the package's foil lining. In addition to the dirty reality of Isabel's humanity and the absurdity of his physical location, Max was now forced to accept the clinical nature of his sexual encounter. It was too much. All of the smells, the harsh realities, swirled inside the poor boy's head until his body ceased to function in a way that would allow him to consummate his lust for Isabel.

This was the beginning of Max's downward spiral. After that moment, not only was it impossible for him to deny there was something wrong with his nose, the trauma of the event had somehow awakened the extraordinary power of his sense of smell. Every locale was now filled with as many scents as the Civic that horrible night. There was no safe haven. His own bedroom was an unbearable source of odor, no matter how much he cleaned. All but the blandest foods were nauseating. Friends, family, and coworkers carried with them a personalized funk that drove Max into seclusion. He spent most of his time alone, in the grassy hills surrounding Lakeview, where he would insert nose plugs, wear a surgical mask, and read comic books.

If I'd known Max at that time, I would have told him that most truly gifted individuals live beyond the parameters and conventions of mainstream society. Van Gogh cut off his ear out of loneliness. Galileo was killed for his heretical ideas. I was once mocked for shunning the senior prom in order to conduct pheromone experiments in the garage. There is a cost for greatness, but, of course, that's difficult to recognize at the age of eighteen.

Max's nose continued to grow, and it was only about two weeks after his date with Isabel that his parents took notice. They said nothing to the boy, thinking it was one final awkward growth spurt. Ed and Kathy Peet were a bit self-conscious about the size of their own noses, and though neither said so outright, each felt perhaps reckless breeding, and not a medical ailment, was the cause of Max's affliction. When September rolled around, Ed and Kathy drove Max to UC Santa Cruz, unaware of their son's medical problem. He'd been a bit testy of late, a bit aloof perhaps, but they thought he was just stir-crazy. The Peets were sure that getting Max out of their house and into the university dorm would help him get back on track.

Max also enjoyed brief illusions of fitting in at college. With the campus so near the ocean, the cool Pacific breeze helped dampen the pungent odors, and make Santa Cruz much more bearable than Lakeview. He even decided to attend his freshman welcome mixer, a radical departure from his previous antisocial mindset.

Dress had become important to Max, given the off-putting appearance of his face. In hopes of drawing Max out of seclusion, Mrs. Peet had purchased him new back-to-school khaki shorts and a UCSC cap he'd pulled down low to hide his overgrown nose. With the smell of the ocean tickling his nostrils, Kleenex stuffed far enough into his nasal passages to avoid detection, and the protective shadow of his cap's brim, Max walked into the courtyard of his freshman dorm with hope. His peers stood grouped around the garden, sipping sodas and munching on tortilla chips. Max felt their eyes on him as he walked to the cooler and fished out a Cherry Coke, but after he'd retrieved his beverage and staked out a spot under a eucalyptus, the onlookers had returned to their conversations.

A young woman approached Max.

"Hi, I'm Amber," she said.

Max panicked. First, because Amber was beautiful; and second, because she was only about five-foot-two, which meant she had a clear view underneath his cap. Max looked at her carefully, checking to see if she was looking him in the eye or staring into the vast blackness of his nostrils.

"I'm Max."

"Hi, Max. Did you know our school mascot is a banana slug? Pretty weird, huh?"

Max noticed that the red hair of her ponytail bounced when she spoke, as if to reinforce the enthusiasm in her high-pitched voice.

"Yeah, I guess."

"Are you from California? I'm not. I'm from Phoenix.

My cousins live in L.A., though. Most people here are from California. I've talked to just about everyone but you, Max."

As she began a monologue about her summer trip to San Diego, Max found it strangely comforting to be bothered by auditory stimuli rather than smell. Still, he was pleased to simply be outside talking with a beautiful young woman who didn't wear perfume or use scented soap. Although she told him she'd already spoken with everyone else at the party, Max imagined the other freshmen looking on with envy as he spoke to Amber.

When Amber finally ceased, Max opened the flip top of his Cherry Coke. He lifted the can toward his lips, a gesture he imagined he would repeat many times over the next year using Coors Light instead of soda. But as he took a sip, Max failed to account for the increased size of his nose. He bumped the top of the can with his enlarged septum and spilled soda down the front of his T-shirt. The liquid splattered against the pavement, causing others to turn and see Max covered in Cherry Coke.

Anyone who's ever been to a cocktail party knows how a good joke can stimulate conversation. Max, standing under the eucalyptus, his new clothes covered in soda, served as the perfect icebreaker for the crowd of nervous freshmen. They laughed uproariously, according to Max, and it's not hard for me to imagine that they probably laughed more heartily than the situation dictated.

While another young man may have smiled and

shrugged, endearing himself to the other newcomers, Max was in such a fragile state that he immediately burst into tears. Amber tried to comfort him and began dabbing his shirt with her napkin. "It's all right, Max. I can get you a straw." But the damage had been done. Two days later someone crossed out the "Peet" on his dorm room nameplate and replaced it with "Beak."

Max's parents didn't know anything was wrong until late October, when Max burst through their front door unannounced, carrying an overstuffed backpack and a small suitcase. Entering the foyer, Max sank to the tile and began crying uncontrollably. He was wet from the rain and wild with rage. The entire Greyhound bus ride he'd only wanted to be somewhere familiar, somewhere where the smells, however awful, were at least predictable. Finding safety in his parents' home, Max's sobbing escalated into unrestrained wailing.

Mrs. Peet admitted she couldn't even ask him what was wrong. Her attention was stuck on his malformed nose, which by this time had grown even larger. "It didn't look natural, almost like a prosthetic," Mrs. Peet would later report. With her boy collapsed in a defeated ball of angst in front of her, she could only think, Is this really my son? What's happened to him? The poor woman was stupefied by his deformity. It was Mr. Peet who walked in from the living room, kneeled down, and said, "What is it? What's wrong, son?"

Max's body shuddered with deep sobs. He raised his head so that his enormous nose was just inches from his father's. Max mustered a look of extreme seriousness, but could not altogether quell his tears. "Chili powder and feet. My roommate smells like chili powder and feet," Max said. The next day, Max officially withdrew from UC Santa Cruz. He moved back in with his parents and began the circuit of doctor visits my patients usually go through before they come to me.

Now you know everything Max revealed to me during our first conversation, plus a bit more. After hearing his story, I took him into the examination room. I knew Max had an enlarged olfactory epithelium before I shone my light into his nostrils and probed his proboscis. It was the only plausible explanation. The examination simply helped quantify his ailment. Max's epithelium measured a full forty-square centimeters, larger than the smelling organ of a bloodhound, larger than any hyper-smeller I'd ever seen.

I'm a scientist, so attaching a measurement to the severity of Max's ailment filled me with a grave sense of responsibility. I realized Max must smell so well that he has a type of sixth sense: an ability to detect slight changes in human emotion, a coming summer rainstorm, the subtleties of exquisite cuisine, and many other things most people can't fathom. What wondrous aromas must make their way daily to Max's olfactory receptors! I was sure that by concentrating a little bit, Max could detect the smell of baking bread from nearby houses, fresh herbs in a neighboring backyard, or the pine forest on the outskirts of town.

The medical profession takes great pains to preserve eyesight and hearing, yet little attention is given to smell. Is it any less important? It has been proven that it is smells we remember, not sights or sounds. Have you ever returned to your old schoolyard only to find it a miniature version of the image held in your mind? But you never forget the smell of the powdered lemonade your mother brought to the beach or the scent of your favorite home-cooked meal simmering on the stovetop. The boy's ailment was surely as much a gift as an affliction. His condition was the olfactory equivalent to x-ray vision.

I sat the boy down in my office once again. We were in the same positions—me behind my large wooden desk and Max slumped in his chair, blond hair covering his face. I told him, as I have already told you, of the localized secretion of growth hormone that was causing both his nose and internal smelling organ to increase in size.

"That's why I can smell everything?"

"Yes, Max."

"Can you make it stop? Can you make me normal again?"

I paused, knowing the statement I was about to make would be brash, beyond the confines of professional conduct, and perhaps selfish. "Yes, I can do that, Max. But I want you to think hard about this. You have the most incredible sense of smell I've ever encountered, perhaps the greatest smelling power of any human who has walked the Earth."

"And that's why I can't be near anyone or anything? What do you have to do to fix it?"

"Now, Max, I can do that, but I want you to think first about what you're giving up. There has to be some upside to your condition, right? Can you not detect things before you see them? Like someone about to come around the corner, or perhaps a cool stream beyond the next hill?"

"It's like everything is on top of me at once. I can't stand it. Even now I can't stand it, your dusty books and your old-man aftershave gel."

"But there must be some good smells too, right?"

Max was now visibly shaken. He held his hands in fists on his thighs. At this point, I believe my frustration overran my professional decorum. I kept prodding, fearing the boy would flee and leave me full of questions. "Can you not detect human emotion? The changing body chemistry that comes with fear? Anger? Happiness? It must be like reading minds!"

"But there are too many smells, too much going on, and the smells get jumbled around. I inhale these things that don't have anything to do with me. I want to be rid of it. I want to smell food and perfumes like a normal person, not body fluids and nasty things miles away. I want you to fix me!"

With this final comment, Max punched his thigh and looked into my eyes with a new seriousness. I knew our conversation was coming to an end. If I pushed harder, I would be testing the boundaries of medical ethics. Still, I could not give in entirely. I told myself my advice would benefit Max, that given time he would learn to embrace his astonishing abilities. However, in retrospect I believe I was acting upon an ambiguous obligation I felt that extended beyond Max. Maybe it was a duty to science, or to humanity, or more likely an unforgiving curiosity that made me want to know just what was possible. Max needed to be pushed, convinced.

"Four weeks, Max. Give it four weeks, and I'll provide you with treatment. In the meantime, I want you to fly home and think about the benefits of your condition. Consider what it would be like to master the most sensitive sense of smell the world has ever known."

In the shadow of his swollen nose, I saw tears welling in Max's eyes. He stood up and walked swiftly out of the room. If he were more courageous, I believe the young man would have screamed at me, or perhaps even thrown my silver-plated nose paperweight across the room. Instead, he showed his defiance by slamming my office door and leaving me with my dust-ridden bookshelves, wood-paneled walls, and gold-framed diplomas.

Even after he'd left, I couldn't stop thinking about him.

I tried to worry about my patient's personal welfare, but instead found myself continually returning to a more self-centered fear about whether or not he would choose to go forward with treatment and destroy his extraordinary olfactory abilities. During the days after our encounter, I constantly wondered if his mindset had changed. I received an answer in the form of an e-mail. It came from a UC Santa Cruz account, so I assumed he'd enrolled for the spring semester. The message read as follows:

> *From: mxPeet@uc.santacruz.edu*
> *To: NozDoc@hotmail.com*
> *Subject: Wish I were well*
>
> *NozDoc,*
>
> *I don't know why you wouldn't fix my nose when I was in DC. Things are worse now, not better like you said. The parties here smell like sex, vomit, and beer. I can't go to my Spanish class because the room smells like French fries. You're right, though; I do have a bit of a sixth sense. I can smell the happiness emitted from people's bodies when I turn my back to leave. I'm a freak. I will gladly trade my new intuition and super-hero nose for a normal life. You may think you're so smart with your cautious approach, but you're not. I'll see you in twelve days, and when I come, I hope you're ready to fix me.*
>
> *-Max*

I was crestfallen. What I'd told Max about his near-limitless potential was completely lost on the boy. My advice had only served to prolong his agony, and I knew his anger was justifiable. It would be impossible for anyone to convince Max of the benefits of his disorder. I grieved for the world's loss and harbored shame for my selfishness. He would be in my office for treatment in just a matter of days, not long enough for a radical shift in thinking or perspective.

I couldn't bear to see the boy when he came back. I made up an excuse about a scheduling overload and had my colleague, Dr. Smithfield, perform the procedure—the injection of the anti-inflammatory—write the prescription for the pills that would halt the flow of growth hormone to Max's olfactory glands, and the referral to the plastic surgeon. Dr. Smithfield said it all went smoothly. He did comment on the severity of Max's disorder, but the extent of the boy's capabilities never occurred to Smitty. Unlike me, he wasn't burdened with imagination.

I liked to pretend Max never came in for treatment, that he was roaming the UC Santa Cruz campus designing the world's perfect perfume, or wowing wine connoisseurs across the Sonoma Valley with his uncanny ability to state vintage years and storage methods without ever taking a sip. I pretended that because of his nose, Max was able to sniff out the perfect mate—that he was lucky in love, never thrown off guard, and successful in his career. I had many for Max. I made him a pastry chef, fireman, forest ranger, psychologist, florist, and an artist. I saw him graduating at the top of his class, accepting the Nobel Prize in middle age, and as alert as ever in his sunset years.

But curiosity can ruin good dreams. Two years after his treatment, I met up with Max. This kind of thing is frowned upon in my profession, but I couldn't help myself. I was in San Francisco for a conference, so I drove a rental car down to Santa Cruz. I had to know if he regretted it, if he missed anything about his extraordinary nose. I needed to know it was really over. To be reminded that it had happened, and that perhaps it could happen again, maybe to someone different, someone who could stand it. Also, there was part of me that wanted to put my guilty conscience to rest and make sure Max was okay after what I'd put him through.

My offer of a free lunch was enough to coax Max into a rendezvous. We met in a Denny's, drank coffee, and stared at each other across an orange-and-brown table. Max was still skinny. His wispy blond hair had grown long and wild. But most striking was the small button nose the plastic surgeon had sculpted onto the boy's face to replace his swollen snout. And pierced through his left nostril was a gold hoop. I stared at the new facial construction at least as long as I'd first studied Max's overgrown nose.

Max was surprisingly friendly. In fact, his demeanor was so amiable I can only assume that the horrible attitude he'd exhibited before was simply a reaction to his medical condition. He acted as though our history was an unfortunate memory of his childhood, something that can even be laughed at in retrospect. Although I suspect the incident was more than that to him, maybe it was too traumatic to relive with true seriousness.

After I felt I'd let the right amount of time lapse, I said, "Do you ever miss it, Max?"

"What? The super snout? No way, man. It was awful. I mean, really awful. After that night with Isabel, I thought I'd never be able to be with a girl again, you know? It was bad."

Max held the syrup canister high over his short stack and let the contents ooze onto his plate.

"But what about the good stuff, discerning human emotions and smelling fresh-cut grass a mile away?"

Max kept his attention on his plate. "It was cool sometimes I guess, but I don't really miss it."

I kept talking, but the boy seemed wholly devoid of nostalgia, devoid of curiosity, devoid of regret. My eyes focused back on his new nose and its jewelry. The conversation was running dry, so I resorted to an easy question. Acting like an old fool, as he might expect, I said, "By the way, nice ring you got there. What made you pierce my favorite sniffer?"

"I don't know. I wanted to try something new. Just wanted to be different I guess."

I looked at my home fries in order to hide my dismay. The scent of the skillet-fried potatoes, onions, and peppers drifted upward to my ordinary smelling organ, and I thought I could detect a hint of paprika. Without looking up, I could hear the sound of Max's cutlery scraping his plate as he sliced into his pancakes and devoured them without a thought.

BURNING BUSH: A CHRISTMAS MIRACLE

She heard his car door slam and braced herself for his brutish presence. She'd rehearsed this conversation all afternoon.

"Christmas traffic by the mall," he grumbled as he walked through the door.

He dropped his briefcase and walked past her toward the kitchen, toward the whiskey. She watched him pour a glass, his bushy eyebrows twisted into a severe scowl. Lately, she couldn't stop looking at them.

"Honey, I need to ask you something," said Mary.

"What?" Dan asked.

She should have waited until he'd hit that spot between his third and fourth drinks. "I want to invite my brother for Christmas."

He exhaled deeply, then returned to the living room and plopped into his recliner. Drink in one hand, newspaper in the other. The recliner had been her gift to him twelve years before, on their first anniversary. Now the fabric of the chair, and the marriage, had worn thin.

"Jesus, Mary," Dan said.

"That's right. And the wise men, and all that."

Dan shoved his paper into his lap, turned toward her, and glared. He did this a lot. He'd garner all his nastiness and direct it into his eyebrows until they pulsed like small, heaving, woodland creatures. He'd tilt them at just the right angle to portray his utter disdain. Over the years, his eyebrows had grown inversely in relation to the strength of their marriage. With both, the marriage and the eyebrows, she hadn't noticed the transmutation until reaching a crisis point.

"He wants to come Thursday," she said. "I talked to him this morning."

"Fine. For Christ's sake." He turned back to his paper.

"Right. Thank you," she said.

Mary smelled the pot roast burning and ran to the kitchen. Too late. Its ends had shriveled. It looked like a deflated football. Thankfully, Dan had no sense of smell. She wouldn't feel his wrath until dinnertime. Maybe she should inject the beef with antifreeze before then.

When Mary returned to the living room, she added, "And he wants to cook Christmas dinner." Dan exhaled and threw his head back against the recliner. Rising above his neatly combed brown hair, she saw the upper ridges of those shaggy eyebrows. She felt old and lonely.

"Roast beef," Dan said.

"You know he won't, Dan." Mary's brother Charles worked as a vegetarian chef. Dan considered this akin to a lifeguard who refused to go into the water.

"I guess we won't be having anyone over then."

"Who did you want to invite?"

"That's not the point."

Mary wasn't sure what the point was, and she didn't

care. She took Dan's empty glass and went to refill it to be sure he'd had three drinks before seeing the pot roast. When bringing the drink to him, she pretended to stroke him affectionately on his brow. Really, she was trying to flatten his unkempt eyebrow with the condensation from the whiskey glass. The renegade hairs bounced back as wild as ever.

Charles returned from the grocery store with loads of plastic bags in each hand. "Hi, hi," he said, and walked into the kitchen to unload. Mary helped. Charles began humming "Jingle Bell Rock." Dan came into the kitchen. He hated humming. He conveyed this to Charles with a careful movement of his left eyebrow. Charles stopped.

"What's on the menu, Charles?" Dan asked.

Charles brought his hands together with a clap. "Missile tofu for the main course."

Dan looked at him quizzically, powerfully.

"Marinated in soy sauce, lime, and hot pepper flakes."

"Ah," said Dan. He got out a tumbler and opened the liquor cabinet. Charles had given him a bottle of small-batch whiskey that morning, but Dan lifted out the Jack Daniels.

Charles had several pans and pots going. Onions sizzled. Water boiled. The exotic aromas filling the house smelled nothing like what Mary produced with her pot roasts and chicken á la king. Mary played sous-chef, chopping and dicing. Charles cooked and hummed. Dan lurked and drank. Mary didn't look at him, but still she knew that his eyebrows moved, pumped up and down like pistons, as he gave her and Charles disapproving looks from the doorway.

"When are we eating?" he asked.

"Almost," said Charles. Mary looked at Dan. He rolled his eyes, then retreated to the living room. A bald spot had replaced the cowlick on the back of his head. His bottom had widened, his shoulders were more round than she remembered. And yes, even from behind, she could see the very tips of his oversized eyebrows peeking out from the sides of his head.

"Mary, watch this pan for me? I've got to make the dressing," said Charles. They switched spots. She swirled the oil and the onions, smelled their delicious aroma, thankful it was something Dan couldn't enjoy. Holding the pan, Mary thought about using its hot underside to flatten her husband's eyebrows. SMACK!

While cooking the onions, Mary decided Dan's sensory defect should be exploited. It was only fair. He'd dominated her for years with his hulking frame, his role as provider, and now with his menacing eyebrows. Then, while she stirred, a plan sprung to mind, a clever, sinister plan. Mary hadn't felt clever in years and because of this she deemed it necessary to galvanize her plan.

She turned off the stovetop, then turned—without

igniting—the gas back on. Charles had his nose in the vinaigrette and didn't notice the scent.

"Dan, can you come here a minute?" Mary asked.

"What?" he said. He entered with heavy steps.

"The pilot light is out," she said.

Charles looked up from his dressing, his nostrils flared, and then his eyes grew wide in horror. Mary shook her head and put her finger to her lips, begging him to stay silent. Charles edged toward the doorway.

"God damn it," said Dan. Whiskey in hand, he removed the pots and pans from the stovetop one by one, clanking them down on the counter. He took a match from the junk drawer. Mary backed up until she was almost in the living room. She pulled Charles over to her and held his arm tight. She wanted him with her. She wanted his consent. Dan approached the stovetop with the lit match.

Mary had loved Dan at one point and for that reason it was only partly enjoyable to watch his whiskey glass explode like a Molotov cocktail. Watching him catch fire ignited a conflagration of emotions. Part of her reveled in the pleasure of having brought such pain upon him, but she also felt sick to her stomach. He hadn't danced since their wedding day, but he danced around the kitchen now. He screamed. He bled. His hair caught fire. He bumped into the walls, leaving burnt skin and blood on the white paint. Had she really meant for this to happen? Was this the outcome she wanted? Dan turned toward her, screaming, his eyes filled with terror, betrayal. His knowing look registered with her, but as she stood face-to-face with him, she focused on his eyebrows, which were completely ablaze. Those hairy, middle-aged-man eyebrows, those furry bushels of contempt, burned on Dan's face. The scene played slowly in Mary's mind. It seemed his eyebrows would burn forever, that she might sit Dan in his recliner and leisurely roast marshmallows over him. And the thought, the hideousness of debasing her husband so that he was simply a heat source for campfire treats, made Mary realize that yes, she had meant for this to happen. She didn't need to feel sick. She could even let out a devious giggle.

Charles ran for a towel and threw it over Dan's head. Dan sank onto the linoleum floor. Smoke billowed from underneath the towel. Dan whimpered. Mary smiled at Charles, and Charles, whose look of horror had faded, seemed almost ready to smile back.

It took fifteen minutes for the ambulance to come, but once Dan had been carted away, Charles finished cooking the missile tofu. Dinner tasted wonderful, largely because Dan wasn't there to criticize it. Of course, Mary knew she wasn't altogether done with him. There'd be legal rigmarole, divorce proceedings. Whatever happened, she was ready. She imagined him across the courtroom, trying his best to appear menacing without the use of his powerful eyebrows.

THE UNWRAPPING PARTY

Half-frozen slush fell from the night sky and a layer of ice spread over the windshield. Robin watched Neil lean close to the glass and flip the wipers on and off. He squinted behind his glasses' thick lenses.

"Jesus," Neil said. "The Miltons picked a hell of a night."

"We're almost there," Robin said. The dashboard clock showed they were twenty minutes late. She picked at the label on the bottle of wine she held in her lap. When she noticed what she'd done, she smoothed it out.

"If I die on the drive over, make sure I'm buried so deep no one can pick me apart at a dinner party in three thousand years," said Neil.

"You know you're curious, Neil," said Robin.

He furrowed his brow as if to make a quip, but said nothing. He'd voiced his opposition at home, and Robin had said it was too late. She'd already told the Miltons they would go.

Robin pulled down the vanity mirror and brushed her bangs to the side with her fingertips. Sometimes her hair fell over her face, making her look like a Saint Bernard. Meredith Milton had her hair styled weekly. It always looked perfect.

"Mummies are things to see in museums or on the Discovery Channel. They're not dinner party entertainment." Neil leaned forward again, his eyes inches from the glass.

He raised his upper lip, exposing his teeth. Hail bounced off the roof of the car in front of them.

"It used to be common in London. Wealthy sophisticates, not unlike ourselves, would throw a party and unwrap a mummy. There are bracelets, pendants, all sorts of treasures hidden inside."

"They also used to charge admission to look at the freaks in mental hospitals," he said.

"We're doing that next weekend," Robin said.

Robin had dressed Neil in a white shirt, no tie, and a gray sport jacket. The men at the country club dressed this way, though the clothes didn't hang right on Neil's narrow, hunched shoulders.

"Where'd she get it again?" Neil asked.

Robin could barely see through the windshield, and she wondered how Neil could carry on a conversation while driving.

"Said her 'Granddaddy picked it up.' Used to be, in Victorian England, they sold them on street corners like soft pretzels."

"It's pretty weird, Robin," he said.

"You know how she is."

Seated across from Robin at a coffee shop, Meredith had talked loudly about the mummy. Others had turned their heads. Meredith seemed not to notice, kept on talking, fingering her pearl necklace, legs crossed, white tennis shoe bouncing in the air. "For God's sake," Meredith had said. "You look like you've caught me smoking in the girls' room." After her loud declaration, several men in line looked over at them, and Robin found it titillating. "The Bennetts are coming too. Yes, the Stevensons and the Bennetts," Meredith added. Robin liked the way the gentile names sounded, and was ashamed of how glad she was to be done with her maiden name.

"Here we are," Neil said. "The Milton mansion."

"Are you sure?" asked Robin. She ran her tongue over her teeth in case of lipstick.

"Yep. 7132. Right there." He pointed to numbers tacked onto the mailbox that only Neil, with his fondness for minutiae, would ever see or think to look for.

An elaborate black metal gate with an M woven into the ironwork guarded the driveway. The gate magically opened. Neil looked at Robin and raised an eyebrow.

The house itself looked like a parody of where the filthy rich live—red brick with white trim, a large circular driveway, and hedges sculpted into neat cubes. Four columns rose from the front porch. This was old money, something about which dot-com millionaires like Robin and Neil knew nothing.

Jack opened the door himself and let out a boisterous "Good evening." Having celebrated his fiftieth birthday the summer before, Jack was a good ten years older than Robin, Neil, and Meredith. Each time Robin saw Jack, he looked taller and fatter, as if he'd grown between encounters. The red hue of his bulbous nose appeared to also have deepened. Jack would likely hand Neil a few drinks throughout the evening, and Robin made careful note of Neil dropping his car keys into his jacket's right pocket.

Robin handed Jack the bottle of wine. "For you."

"Ah ha!" Jack said, holding the bottle at eye level and studying the label. Robin wanted to know whether the exclamation meant he approved of her selection, but Jack simply took their coats and said, "Pretty hellish out there, isn't it?" The sound of falling ice rattled against the Miltons' brick fortress.

"It's the mummy's curse," Meredith said as she entered the foyer. She wore a loose-fitting, white linen dress with full-length sleeves and carefully torn fringe at the hem. "Do you like it?" she asked, holding out her arms and twirling. "I thought it was appropriately ghastly." The slit up the side exposed her pale, thin legs and made Robin realize that Meredith was past her prime. Robin gave her dinner party giggle. "You look absolutely macabre."

"Yes, well, Mere is very excited. She's spent the whole week researching mummies and coming up with reasons why it's okay to destroy one," Jack said.

"Well it is Granddaddy's mummy," Meredith said, hands on her hips, a debutante pout.

"You're absolutely right, dear," Jack said. He gave Neil a jovial slap on the shoulder. Then, leaning close, he said, "I'd rather think of all that's wrong with it and do it anyway." Jack gave Neil a wink, then straightened to address them all. "Who wants a drink?" He led them into the parlor, where they sat in large, leather chairs, cocktails in hand——Scotch for Jack, cranberry and vodka for Meredith and Robin, and a rum and Coke with lots of lime for Neil. When the phone rang, Meredith rushed to the kitchen to answer it. She returned and said, "That was the Bennetts. They can't come. All the streetlights are out over there and Nebraska Avenue is shut down. It took them a half-hour just to drive to the end of their block, then turn around and go home."

"Oh, what a shame," said Robin, trying to sound sincere.

"Yes, it really is," said Meredith. She paused for a moment, looking past them all.

Jack rattled his ice cubes. "Well, let's quit waiting and eat," he said. He stood up. The others followed him into the spacious dining room, lit by candles held in an array of candelabra. In the dim, flickering light, oil paintings looked like hollow portraits encased in glistening frames. A deep-red-colored tablecloth covered the oak table. In place of wine glasses, silver goblets sat beside each place setting.

Neil said, "No dry ice?"

Jack guffawed. "I'm telling you, she went overboard."

"I like it," Robin said. "It's like Halloween."

"It's better than Halloween," Meredith said. "It's the dead of winter."

"Yes. 'It was a dark and stormy night,'" said Robin.

"It's deader. Colder. Icier," said Meredith.

"Well, I have to admit, you've got me going," Neil said. "A few more minutes listening to you, a couple more goblets of wine, and I'll be ready to uncover the mysteries of the mummy."

"We're having eye of newt as an appetizer, followed by a generous serving of seasoned bat wings," Jack said.

"Oh shush," Meredith said to her husband, waving her hand. Turning to her guests, she continued, "We're having Cornish game hens with roasted potatoes. I had Rosie cook them before she left for the evening, so don't thank me. They're just heating in the oven." Meredith went to the kitchen and emerged with plates of food, which she set in front of her guests.

Neil worked at his hen like he was lifting toothpicks with a pair of tweezers. Robin was fairly certain he'd never eaten Cornish game hen. Small bones hid within the meat and carefully seasoned skin. Robin found the taste pleasant enough, though hardly worth the effort.

"Rosie, this dinner is just divine!" Meredith said to no one.

"It is very good," Robin said.

Neil looked quizzically at his plate, then took a sip of wine. Next, he paused, his expression frozen as if he were suddenly struck by a bad memory. The action was so noticeable it required comment.

"A goose walk over your grave?" Meredith asked.

Robin tried to think of something to say to draw attention away from Neil. Jack, his mouth full of potatoes, did it for her. "For Christ's sake, Mere," he said. "Let the man eat his bird." He smiled at Robin while chewing and held his fork upright as if preparing to bang its butt on the tabletop. Robin couldn't decide whether to be repulsed or impressed by the masculine, grease-smacking noises Jack made while chewing. His manner held a ridiculous macho appeal.

"I do have to admit, Meredith, this atmosphere you've created is quite extraordinary. If there was ever an environment that would make me want to pick apart the dead, this is it," Neil said. Robin gave him a scolding look.

"Why thank you, darling," Meredith said. This isn't an everyday occurrence for us. I had to go all-out. I had to invite our most ghoulish friends."

Robin smiled too deeply, and looked down at her plate.

After dinner, Meredith led them into the attic with one of the garish candelabrum. Her Morticia-Adams-style dress flowed behind her on the stairway. Exposed wooden beams and a tall, peaked ceiling gave the attic a spacious feel. In the center of the space, a table had been erected using saw-horses and a flat board. What Robin presumed to be the mummy lay covered by a white sheet.

"Ah, I see you've arranged a grand unveiling," Neil said.

"Oh, of course, dear," Meredith said. "This is a magnificent event."

Strewn about the deep crevices of the attic were generations of dead Miltons' discards. Old furniture, some shrouded in white cloth, and cardboard boxes befittingly covered with dust made Robin feel as though even the disarray had been carefully arranged. A floor lamp in the corner lit the room. Meredith had draped an elaborate red-and-gold cloth over the lampshade so that it cast an eerie glow across the mummy's white covering. Meredith placed her candelabrum on an old wicker table. She walked over to the body with her arms extended and legs stiff at the knee, mocking the limited mobility of the monster-movie mummy. Her white dress helped. Upon reaching the table, she grabbed the sheet between her thumb and forefinger and said, "Ladies and gentlemen, this evening we are going to discover things no one has seen for thousands of years. This is not for the faint of heart. You may be disgusted by the look of death upon this ancient face. You may be awestruck by the beautiful relics of a grand civilization. You may encounter something you never predicted, never could have imagined. The mysteries waiting inside this mummy are unknown to all of us."

Purposely theatrical, Meredith's speech quieted her audience. Robin certainly believed the endeavor required a certain amount of austerity. Outside, sleet pattered against the roof like dirt atop a coffin. Within the attic, the candelabrum's light flickered and cast quick-moving shadows across faces.

Meredith lifted the sheet like a magician unveiling a woman sawed in half. The sarcophagus was small, a little over five-feet long. Chipped paint on the exterior made it appear more authentic than a well-preserved museum piece. The painted figure's large round eyes seemed out of proportion, almost cartoonish. Jewels had been painted on the wood using dull yellow, instead of royal gold. Until this point, it hadn't occurred to Robin that in addition to mummifying pharaohs, ancient Egyptians had preserved commoners.

"Give me a hand, Neil," Jack said. He and Neil lifted the top half of the sarcophagus and placed it against the wall next to the Miltons' discarded furniture. Next, they lifted the body out of the sarcophagus well and laid it on the table. They moved the sarcophagus off the table, so only the body lay atop the sheet. Strips of thick cloth coiled around the body to form a cocoon. Together, Jack and Neil removed the outer layer of wrapping until the outline of a human body took shape.

"Is it a man or a woman?" asked Robin. The mummy's sunken eyes and the small bridge of its nose looked as if sculpted from clay. The mouth had been left uncovered——something Meredith said was abnormal, and its teeth were fully intact, giving the impression it was capable of speech.

"I don't know. It could be either, or perhaps neither, like Akhenaton," Meredith said.

Robin considered Meredith's comment akin to name-dropping at a cocktail party.

"What does it feel like?" asked Robin.

Jack stood staring at the mummy. Neil answered, "Kind of like dried clay. It's chalky, but it reminds you of once having been wet."

"Like the chalk lines on a baseball field," Jack added.

Neil nodded, but Robin knew he'd never been close to a ball field.

"You can touch it," Meredith said. "Go ahead."

Robin reached for the corpse's skull. She found a loose bandage end and unraveled a piece that'd been looped around the forehead. As she pulled the cloth from the ancient body, it made a ripping sound. She stopped.

"Should I keep going?"

Meredith shooed her on with a flick of her wrist. Jack reached over to hold the mummy's head off the table, and Robin slowly unwrapped the bandage. Just five long strips covered the skull, and once they'd been removed, the body looked horrifically human. Gray skin lay tight against the bone, and long wisps of wiry black hair clung to the scalp. Robin knew she'd have to be careful not to let the brittle neck snap as she continued.

Neil stood over the table staring at the mummy's face, as if in a trance.

"What should I do with these?" Robin asked, holding up the bandages.

Meredith shrugged, and Robin dropped them at her feet. Their voices and bodies were still, and the silence made the heavy beating of hail sound as if it were mocking the quiet within the house. Then Robin said, "Neil, you should try it." Neil was squeamish, but she wanted him to appear eager. Neil gave her a fake, knowing smile, and took hold of the mummy's right hand. The mummy's knotty finger joints looked like fruit tree branches. Robin wondered if Neil recognized the similarity and whether it made his task easier. As he tore a bandage on the mummy's thumb, a puff of dust rose, and the rigid body creaked. Neil dropped the mummy's hand and jolted backward. Robin glanced over at Jack, who covered a smile with his hand.

Neil didn't look up. He grasped the shriveled hand again and continued unwrapping the thumb, then the forefinger, then the middle finger. He worked with delicacy around the shriveled paw's digits, brow furrowed and his head bowed close to his working fingers. This is how he looked when rebuilding the gadgetry inside his computers.

Neil found the group's first relic—an elaborate gold ring with diamond studs along its edges. Still on the dead hand, the gems refracted the red glow of the lamplight. Neil pulled the ring off the lifeless knuckle and held it in front of his face.

"It looks like it could have come wrapped in a Tiffany's

box," Robin said. No tarnish, no scratches. Jack took it from Neil and held it to the light.

"This is a real beauty. What do you think, love?" Jack said.

Meredith turned pale, her mouth agape. Robin noticed her fingering the diamond pendant around her neck. Her gaze fixed on the ring.

"What is it, Mere?" Jack asked.

"That's not an Egyptian ring."

"Of course it is. How else would the mummy come to wear it?" Jack said.

"The Egyptians didn't have diamonds like that," Meredith said.

"Well, this guy did," Jack said, pointing to the mummy. Robin and Neil leaned close to Jack, and he opened his hand to give them a look at the ring. The gold band twisted around itself in an elaborate serpentine design. Finely cut diamonds arranged with laser-like symmetry spanned the length of the band. The edges had been faceted with exactness impossible to achieve by hand, and though reluctant to give credence to Meredith's flabbergast reaction, Robin also began to wonder whether this was indeed an ancient artifact.

Robin knew Meredith would go to great lengths to heighten the notoriety of her dinner parties. An expert could have been called in to make things appear authentic, to age the bandages. But the surprise on Meredith's face seemed authentic.

Robin next imagined the ring had perhaps been a gift from an old lover, that Jack had discovered Meredith's affair and somehow stuffed the ring into the mummy. However, Jack looked unaffected by the ring's appearance. If he'd been watching a sinister plan come to fruition, he'd have shown some satisfaction.

Robin remembered a lunch date with Meredith at Casa del Taco when, after a couple margaritas, Meredith had swiped the metallic cowboy napkin holder from the table and stuffed it into her purse. "A little souvenir from our afternoon," she said with a drunken smile. Robin had been astonished and could think of nothing to say. She'd forced a smile. Months later she saw the Tex-Mex centerpiece on the dining room table at Meredith's Cinco de Mayo party. "I picked it up last spring in New Mexico," Robin had overheard Meredith tell a guest.

Maybe this ring was a greater indiscretion, an item Meredith pocketed while the clerks at Tiffany's circled about behind the counter. Maybe it'd belonged to another matron among Washington's elite. There'd been a fund-raiser, a party of some sort, and while the hostess entertained guests in the downstairs dining room, Meredith had been upstairs under the guise of using the powder room. She'd gone into the hostess's bedroom and rifled through her jewelry box. Robin imagined Jack driving Meredith home, the couple recapping the party and all its shortcomings while Meredith reached into her purse and ran her fingertips over the salacious diamonds.

Robin took the ring from Jack. "It's really quite extraordinary," she said. She turned and saw Meredith wide-eyed. Slowly, Meredith reached over the decrepit body and took the ring from Robin. She placed it at the foot of the mummy.

"Why don't we see what else is under here?" Meredith said. Her eyes looked down and the tendons in her neck showed distinctly as she swallowed.

"Well, I suppose we can divvy up the booty at the end of the evening," Robin said. Her sonorous voice had the desired effect of alleviating some of the weight that had fallen over the group.

Meredith also acted the part. "Jack, honey, why don't you continue? There could be a monogrammed cigar lighter in there for you, dear."

Despite her smile, Robin saw Meredith's eyes tearing up.

"Yes, well, let's see what else your granddad hid in this old piñata," said Jack. His gruff masculinity failed to cover his apprehension. Standing near the mummy's feet, Jack started to unwrap a heel. Rigid tendons stretched across the top of the foot and pushed against the dried, gray skin. The mummy's toes had been individually wrapped. Jack kept unraveling and allowed the path of the bandage to take him up the mummy's calf. The sleek outline of its tibia showed clearly, curving slightly with the ascent of Jack's hands. The bandage grew increasingly wide, the unwrapping moving quickly, and Jack cupped his hand under the mummy's knee so he could lift its thin leg and remove the dressing. Inside the dusty folds, Jack found a small key. He rubbed it with his thumb, and the bandages' grit and age fell away.

"What the hell is this, Mere?" Jack said.

"I don't know what it is, Jack. I didn't put it there."

It looked like a regular house key. Schlage brand with a dab of green paint.

"Mere, this is your thing, right? This whole mummy business. What the hell is it doing with this key, huh? Can you explain that?"

She stammered before speaking, "There's a legend I read about. About stolen mummies. How the thieves get . . ."

Jack threw his hands in the air, and Meredith quieted and retreated a step. Robin wondered if he'd ever hit her.

"The hell with the legend, Mere. What's going on?"

"I didn't do anything." She fought back tears. "The legend says the thieves' secrets come; that things can be found."

"Oh, Jesus! Shut up, Mere," said Jack.

Robin wished she could run back down the narrow staircase. She looked over to Neil who was drawing imaginary lines with his forefinger on the white tablecloth and watching, through side-glances, the Miltons squabble.

Jack shifted his accusing stare from Meredith to the

mummy. He removed the key with care and appeared to be trying hard to avoid contact with the corpse's wrinkled, chalky skin.

Meredith had told Robin about Jack's affairs. For Meredith, it was an accepted, though troubling, element of his persona. Jack was respectfully secretive, but sometimes he'd slip up and Meredith would find suspicious receipts or overhear cryptic phone conversations. Robin didn't understand the arrangement, but that's the way Jack and Meredith did it. Meredith knew Jack loved her and would never leave. If the key were a woman's house key, it would be against the rules. Too intimate.

Standing over the mummy, Jack studied the key. He looked at Meredith. She stared at him intently, as if begging him to speak, but he didn't say anything. Jack placed the key on the table next to Meredith's ring, his face suggesting the same heaviness Meredith's had shown a moment before. He looked at Neil, then at Robin, and gave a snorting laugh.

"I don't know what the hell a mummy is doing with this. What's going on, Mere?"

"The mummy will punish and shame its desecrators, the story said."

"Shut up! Please!" said Jack.

The room was eerily silent before Robin said, "I've got to say, Meredith, this is not at all what I was expecting." Her party voice again, meant to get the group back into a lighter mood.

Hail now pounded the attic roof with an unrelenting beat. Robin wished for thunder, or perhaps gusts of wind, anything to disturb the steady drumming. Its constancy accentuated their silence.

"Robin, why don't you have another go?" Jack said, waving a hand at her.

His grin almost a sneer. Robin wondered if her manufactured pleasantness irked him.

She forced a smile. "All right, Jack," she said and moved over to the mummy's right arm. She carefully unwrapped its hand and forearm. She moved with less trepidation this time. She leaned close to the mummy, her lips pursed, her fingers working quickly. The length of bandage ended at the shoulder, and the humerus head showed clearly through the tight skin. Robin dropped the gray-brown lengths of cloth to the floor, and the four of them looked at the naked limb.

"Nothing hidden on that one," Neil said.

"Yes. I'm still hoping for a beautiful Egyptian ruby," Robin said. Jack's head snapped toward her, an expression of disdain, and she looked down at the body.

With much of the mummy now exposed, it looked to Robin more like a gruesome dead body than a preserved artifact.

"Neil?" Meredith asked, gesturing toward the mummy.

Neil walked around the table to the right leg. He took hold of the bandage gingerly and began unwrapping at the ankle. Even on his second time around, the color left his face and he grew deathly pale, except for splashes of red on each cheek.

"Atta boy, Neil," Jack said. Already Jack was falling back into character.

Neil flinched when the bandage yanked at the mummy's crusted knee joint, causing the whole body to jostle. The bandage ripped loose, and a puff of dust rose in the muted lamplight.

"Tear it open, big boy," Jack said.

Neil grabbed hold of the mummy's knee to stabilize it as he pulled at the linen. The mummified skin looked gritty, like it'd been rubbed in coal. Robin thought it would help if Neil could think of the body this way: dirt, minerals. She wanted him to show he wasn't just a nerdy software engineer, but a red-blooded American like Jack. If he could do this, the Miltons might see that Neil was fit to sail in the Hamptons and drive a golf cart while smoking a fat cigar. She hoped they didn't notice how he squinted, the way his nose crinkled in concentration as he unearthed the next object.

Pressed tightly against the thigh, Neil found a tarnished coin. He peeled it away from the mummified skin and held it in his palm. Meredith and Jack leaned in for a look.

Robin was the one who, this time, inhaled deeply. Her

eyes widened, and she stepped back. Neil reached out to hand her the coin, and she picked it off his palm as if it were about to crumble. Then, she looked at it closely, inspecting it the same way Meredith had examined her ring.

It had been her grandfather's. Dated 1783. She saw the scratch across the face of the stoic Indian, the scratch the coin dealer had said made it worth only a couple hundred dollars. When she and Neil were just married, it was the only thing she owned of value, and she'd kept it hidden in a flip-up jewelry box in her sock drawer. Neil had just started his business and spent most of the day hunched over a computer, screwdriver in hand, in the garage. He'd come inside to eat and pontificate about his grandiose ideas and how rich they'd be, but they weren't rich. Robin had worked extra hours when she could. She clipped coupons. She bought second hand. At night, she'd get out her grandfather's half-cent and wonder how much she could get for it. Neil didn't notice their poverty until the electric company shut off their power. "Now what? I can't work!" he'd said. Without telling him, she sold the coin. He didn't ask how she'd gotten the power turned back on, almost like he'd attributed it to some act of God, a turn of good fortune. Robin hadn't truly forgiven him for it, even now. She wasn't supposed to have sold the coin. In California, she'd told the story to her friend Margaret. It was a rags-to-riches tale that, in the West, made her endearing. It was not a story for Meredith and Jack.

Robin closed her hand around the coin and reached to where her jean pocket should have been, before remembering she was wearing a dress. She held the cool copper tightly.

"All right," Jack said. "Let's play 'em straight. That key is mine. It won't shock any of you. I can say that because, Meredith, the ring has something to do with you, though Lord knows I didn't give it to you. Robin, you got the scandalous coin. Neil, my boy, that leaves you."

"Okay," Neil said. He looked down at the mummy, doubtlessly wondering where to start.

"I mean, I don't know what my wife is up to here, but we might as well play along," Jack said.

Meredith balled her hands into fists and straightened her arm, her knuckles white. "Jack, I didn't do a damn thing to this mummy," Meredith said. She stared at him, her eyes ready to fill with tears. Robin gazed toward the ceiling and shifted her attention to the unrelenting hail slapping against the rooftop. Everyone was silent except for a small sniffle from Meredith. Jack looked up, too. His trance broke when he turned toward the sound of bandages being pulled from the withered body. Neil went to work, this time unwrapping the mummy's torso.

He ripped at the body with reckless speed. Instead of propping it up to get around to the back, Neil tore at pieces of wrapping on the chest.

"Let me help you there, Neil," Jack said, and he went over and gently held and tilted the mummy's skull.

"Well I guess it isn't going to a museum or anything," Meredith said. Given the series of inexplicable events that had transpired, the statement was mundane. She tried too hard.

Neil worked crudely, and Robin wondered if it were in part by design. They'd expected squeamishness and delicacy, but wasn't he the one tearing at the bandages for the third time? She hoped the Miltons recognized his bravado. Macho Jack, though now holding the body, had yet to peel the linens from the dead skin. The grit of the bandages' adhesive and the skin's flaking top layer hadn't gotten under his fingernails. If Neil could only go fast enough, unwrap all of it, maybe he would find his own secret. Robin couldn't imagine what it could be, but she wanted him to have one. Something dark, sinister even, impressive.

The problem was Neil was earnest, one of his most endearing and aggravating qualities. Robin watched him, rooted for him, but no matter how sinister he looked ripping and tearing at the dead body, she couldn't help but think there was no darkness within him to uncover. The curse of which Meredith had spoken hadn't accounted for the possibility that a mummy might be desecrated by a mild-mannered engineer.

Having laid bare the mummy's chest and back, Neil stopped unwrapping. Jack gently lowered the mummy so that it was flush against the table. The dried skin clung tightly to bone, leaving the elaborate outline of the rib cage. A long, stitched incision ran along the left side of the torso, and the mummy's arms and legs appeared now connected to an entire human body. Even the dead face seemed to have picked up an expression. Its hollow eyes stared. Shriveled lips, shrunken gums, and crooked teeth formed an upturned smirk.

"I guess there's nothing else in there, Neil," Jack said.

Neil looked at Robin, then at Meredith and Jack. The Miltons each wore a gentle smile, the kind passers-by give small children. Robin regretted coming. The Bennetts should have been there instead.

"There's nothing there, Neil," said Robin.

Neil looked down at the body. Its skin appeared green under the room's red light, and its head seemed to have shifted on its decrepit neck. The ribs looked so small, like delicate twigs, and the skin had dried paper-thin.

Standing over the mummy, Neil strained his jaw into a hideous grimace, raised his fist, and drove it through the chest. The sound of cracking bone echoed off the attic's exposed beams. Dust spewed from the open cavity and billowed into the air. The odors of rotten sawdust and mummifying salts spread with the aerated dust, and Robin covered her nose with her hand. Through the haze, she could see Neil reaching into the mummy's chest, ripping out handfuls of linens and more sawdust.

"Neil, stop!" she yelled at him. But he couldn't. He tore at it foolishly.

Jack grabbed his arm. "Stop. That's enough," he said. Neil clawed clumsily at the body with his other hand, before Jack subdued him by grabbing him at the elbows.

"There's got to be something else in there. You all had things in there." He was almost pleading with Jack, then he looked at Robin. "I didn't find anything."

Meredith pulled out a dust-covered chair and slid it toward Neil. He sat slumped in it like a defeated boxer. His chest heaved, and his eyes focused on Robin. Dust settled around them. No one spoke, and they were again left listening to the chorus of hail, this time mixed with the sound of Neil's heavy panting. The smell of the mummy's innards permeated the room as waves of particulates drifted through Meredith's eerie lighting.

Meredith dragged a metal washtub across the floor, over to the mangled body. With both hands she grabbed a heap of linen and dumped it into the tub. Jack walked away from Neil to help. He picked bone fragments from the table and swept up sawdust with the edge of his hand. Neil watched from his chair, his heavy breathing in rhythm with the pounding outside.

With the scraps piled in the basin, only the desecrated carcass remained on the table. Jack lifted it and placed it headfirst into the oval, metal tub. He jammed in the skull and allowed the legs to protrude.

Jack retreated a few steps to the white-clothed table, picked up the key, and threw it underhand into the basin, where it settled with the scraps of the mummy.

"What was that anyway, Jack," asked Meredith in an almost inaudible voice.

"Do you want to tell me about that ring?"

Meredith shook her head.

Meredith retrieved her diamond ring from the table. She looked at it again and, like Jack, tossed it into the tub. Robin picked up her grandfather's coin and rubbed its face with her thumb. She felt the chalky residue of the mummy's body. The half-cent's sudden appearance was unnatural. She also dropped it into the tub. Neil took the white sheet from the table and laid it over the mangled body. Jack gave Neil a paternal pat on his shoulder.

Shrouded in the white tablecloth, the mummy now looked like the rest of the covered artifacts littering the attic. If they were to push the washtub against the back wall next to the discarded furniture, no one would ever notice the mummy. Meredith blew out the dancing flames of the candelabrum, then walked over to the lamp and removed the red cloth. Bright light washed over the attic, the dark corners of the room stark and conspicuous.

They left after kisses on the cheek and the rounding up of jackets, and everyone pretended they would get together again.

LITTLE MISS STRANGE

Brad nodded toward the corner booth. I turned to look, and Little Miss Strange glowered at me through the hazy light. Her devilish, green-yellow eyes narrowed to slits. I quickly turned away embarrassed and hit Brad on the shoulder, hoping that she would know my staring had been Brad's fault.

Brad laughed. "Jesus, L.M. What the fuck?"

Brad was a whiz with nicknames. L.M. was short for Lil' Mike, a name he'd derived by combining his affinity for hip-hop, my skinny frame, and my name, Mike. Brad loved it, even after I pointed out that a nickname should reduce the number of syllables.

He'd come up with Little Miss Strange too, from the Hendrix song, for the skinny, wild-haired, black-clad blonde who camped out in the corner booth of the bar across from our Connecticut Avenue office. A few days after he'd christened her, she wore a black Hendrix T-shirt. Brad nearly went ape shit with delight. A week later she wore a 50 Cent shirt. Brad didn't comment, but I found it difficult to reconcile.

Brad chuckled and said, "What you so pissed off about anyway, L.M.?" He undid the top button of his baby-blue dress shirt, took a swig of his Corona, and motioned to the bartender for another.

Most of what I knew about Miss Strange I'd gathered through side-glances while walking past her to the bathroom or from Brad's observations gleaned from his walks to the "pisser." It was hard to get a good look at her in the dim recesses of the bar. Sometimes she appeared young, in her early twenties, like me. Other times, I'd peer beneath her wild mop of hair and see deep wrinkles along the sides of her mouth, crow's feet around her eyes. Her long, thin nose cast a narrow shadow across her face. She wore a barrage of metallic bracelets, which spiraled up her forearms like armor. Her clothes, though they changed with the season, were always black. Of course I never admitted it to Brad, but I thought she exuded sex.

I looked at my watch. Seven o'clock. I wanted to leave soon, before the happy-hour crowd turned into the Friday-night crowd and I ended up out for the evening with Brad. I had to pee first though, and I'd need to pass Miss Strange to get to the bathroom. Upon my return, Brad would want a full report about what I saw when I passed her. He might even order another round. Still, I had to go.

"Brad," I said. "I've got to go to the pisser." He didn't realize I was mocking him.

A waitress stood in the aisle and served as a shield, allowing me an inconspicuous glance as I slipped past Miss Strange's booth. She was looking down at a book on her table. Her hair covered her face, but I noticed her hands. Black nail polish. Thumb rings.

I emerged from the restroom, stepped into the bar, and stood for a moment. People in jeans, rolled-up sleeves, and unbuttoned collars packed the room. Happy hour was over. I looked at the back of Miss Strange's head and noticed red streaks in her blonde hair. Already, I'd decided not to look at her as I passed. My coordination had deteriorated, and I needed to focus on weaving through the crowd. Also, I was scared of her. I looked for Brad's head jutting out of the crowd, but didn't see him.

Walking toward the bar, I heard a voice behind me. "Your buddy's gone."

I turned around. Her eyes locked on mine.

Neither Brad nor I had talked to her before. "Excuse me?"

"Your buddy. He started talking to this cheerleader type and left with her and her friends."

She chewed gum. I heard it pop against her teeth. She moved her jaw slowly from side-to-side like she was working tobacco. Her thin nose matched her angular cheekbones and pointed chin. I guessed she was probably my age, maybe a little older, though delicate wrinkles trickled from the corners of her mouth and eyes. Maybe she was a smoker. It would explain her gravelly voice.

"Oh. Thanks," I said. My stomach turned sour. I began to sweat. I thought about what it would be like to undress her. I turned to leave.

"Why do you hang out with him, anyway?" she said.

I turned back toward her. "He's a coworker. We go for drinks sometimes."

"He's an asshole," she said.

"You don't know him," I said. It had come out wrong. I'd spoken out of surprise, but it sounded like I was defending him.

"Sorry," she said. Her eyes softened, and she looked down at her hands. Then, she said, "Is he an asshole?"

"Yeah. He kind of is." I smiled. A forced smile because I was still scared of her. The sleek contours of her neck moved gracefully into her black T-shirt.

"Gotta get through here," someone yelled. I turned to see an aggravated waitress behind me carrying a tray of beers. I leaned my rump into the booth seat opposite Miss Strange so the waitress could get past.

Miss Strange stood, reached out, and gently pulled me down by the sleeve of my casual-Friday Polo shirt. "Sit down," she said. I looked at her across the table. Brad would never believe it, but I was already thinking I'd never tell Brad.

"What's your name?" she asked.

A book lay facedown on the tabletop. It took me a minute to read the title upside down, but it was a biography of Billy the Kid. "Mike," I said.

She replied with, "huh," but didn't offer her name, so I asked her.

"What do you call me?" she asked.

"I'm sorry?" I said. Momentarily, I believed Miss Strange possessed psychic powers.

"You come in here every couple weeks. Your buddy stares at me like an idiot, you give sideways glances, and then you whisper. I assume you have a revolting nickname for me."

Because she already seemed to know about it, I felt okay telling her. "Little Miss Strange," I said. "Like the Hendrix song. Brad, he's the one who thought of it."

"That's Noel Redding's song, though it's Hendrix on guitar."

I grunted in affirmation, but had nothing to say in return. She took a sip of water, then said, "Hendrix, he's another lefty."

"What?" I said.

"He was left-handed," she said. "So was Billy the Kid." She pointed to her book with a ballpoint pen hooked in her left hand. "Both outlaws."

I gave her a quizzical look. I've got one down where I intentionally skew my eyebrows to invite further explanation. This launched her into a soliloquy on famous lefties—Leonardo Da Vinci, H.G. Wells, Bill Clinton, Julius Caesar, Joan of Arc, Mark Twain, Paul Klee, and Babe Ruth. To her, their handedness had lead to their success. Being right-handed, I'd never paid much attention to lefties, but she spoke with such gusto, gesticulating with her slender arms, smiling, her eyes growing wide, that I believed maybe lefties were extraordinary. She recounted dates of ancient battles and ERAs of Cy Young Award winners. She must have gone to college. I pictured her in black sweats, curled up like a snake in a chair near the back of a university lecture hall.

Sometimes I asked questions, but the conversation never settled on either of us. We discussed Napoleon's leadership qualities and how perhaps his arrogance was an asset. This led to a discussion of the cocky, talented, and left-handed Ty Cobb. From there we talked about Cary Grant. She didn't wait for segues, but instead spilled information as if it were of vital importance.

Miss Strange sipped water, and I, feeling pressure from the wait staff, ordered beers. When I checked my watch, it was nearly eleven. I'd been drinking slowly since five-thirty. I started thinking, again, of an exit strategy. I wanted Miss Strange to come with me, but didn't know how to broach the subject. There was never a break in conversation. Plus, I didn't know her name.

She preempted me. "Let's get out of here," she said, and she gave me a sultry look, which surprised me because our conversation had never gotten flirtatious. Then, she stood up. I paid my tab at the bar while she stood by the door gripping her Billy the Kid biography, her intense eyes peering past the crowd like she was somewhere else.

We headed up Connecticut Ave toward R Street. I worked hard to walk straight and to enunciate clearly. She talked about H.G. Wells, "a real visionary," who wrote about rockets and time travel half a century before the right-handed Ray Bradbury. The brisk, November night helped sober me. I wanted to know where we were going but stayed silent and followed. She moved her pale, slender, bare arms as she talked. It must have been below fifty degrees, but she didn't have a jacket. She glided over the sidewalk in eerie grace, and though I peered at her face, I still could not see her clearly. She seemed to dispel the street lamps' light.

Finally, I said, "Where are we going?"

"My place," she said.

We turned down a narrow street of brick sidewalks packed with parked cars and dimly lit townhouses. A fog rolled through the city, uncharacteristic for that time of night. She didn't say anything about it, and we moved through like we were wading across a river. I wanted to ask her name, but started to wonder if maybe she'd already said it. Maybe I'd forgotten. I couldn't very well ask her now. Still, I knew I might sleep with her, and I wasn't the kind of guy who slept with a girl without knowing her name. In fact, I'd only slept with one other girl before. Her name was Elizabeth.

We arrived at her townhouse somewhere northeast of Dupont Circle. I hadn't paid attention to how we'd gotten there. I followed her up the front steps. "My roommates are all out," she said, and she unlocked the iron gate in front of the door.

Inside, the house smelled like dust. There were no shoes by the door, no magazines about, no dirty dishes, no evidence of roommates. She led me into the living room and over to a black leather couch. I sat. She went into the kitchen. Stacks of unpacked boxes cast long shadows around the room.

She came back and handed me a glass of water. "Sorry about the boxes," she said. "I just moved in."

I nodded and took a sip, but I knew Brad and I had been watching her for months. Another look at the boxes showed some were stained on the bottom. A green liquid leaked out of the corner of one and pooled on the rug.

Miss Strange sat sidesaddle on the couch beside me. Her skirt rode high, and she gently stroked her calf with the fingertips of her left hand. Despite my alcohol intake, I felt an erection growing. She smiled. Her eyes looked more cat-like than they had in the bar. She leaned in to kiss me, and I knew this was my one chance. She wouldn't like me tomorrow. I was too ordinary. She gripped my shoulder. Her nails dug into my skin through my shirt. She stopped, her face inches from mine, and I could feel her breath warm on my cheek, too warm, like steam. She smelled slightly rotten. She licked my lips with her tongue.

Suddenly, I became dizzy. Her face appeared to be swaying from side-to-side. The last thing I remember was looking at my water glass and thinking it had to be the explanation. Something was in the water. I silently scolded myself for coming home with her, then closed my eyes. In the darkness, I heard Miss Strange say, "Let me come in, Mike."

*

A hard rain woke me. She'd deposited me on Connecticut Avenue, right in front of the bar we'd left the night before. I righted myself by leaning against the building. My watch said seven forty-five, and the sun fought its way through gray clouds. The sporadic, Saturday morning traffic whizzed past on wet asphalt.

Drenched, I walked south toward the Metro. I tried hard to remember what had happened, but only recalled passing out on Miss Strange's couch. I'd had a dream too. Miss Strange had tied me to a chair in a wood-paneled parlor, cut off my right hand while laughing demonically, then slurped the blood out of it. When done, she'd tossed my severed hand over her shoulder. I'd screamed and begged, but she'd insisted it was for the best. Trying to remember more only hurt my head, and I thought again about my glass of water.

When I got to the turnstile, I pulled out my wallet. Usually, I whipped out my fare card with one hand. This day, I wasn't so dexterous and needed two. On the station platform, white- and blue-collar workers looked fresh in clean clothes, ready for a Saturday job. A couple dirty, mussy-haired types sat slumped on benches, including a green-hued young woman with a stain on the shoulder of her black jacket. I probably looked as bad.

When the train came, I hunkered down in the back row of the last car. Closing my eyes helped my headache. I held my hands in my lap and feeling queasy I loosened my belt. I did this with my left hand, and silently congratulated myself for suddenly regaining coordination. When I got off the train, I took out my fare card with one hand—my left again.

As I walked from the Court House Metro Station to my apartment, I started testing the abilities of my right hand versus those of my left. I tried snapping. The noise echoed in my left hand but was barely perceptible with my right. I wrote my name in the air. Seemed okay with both hands. I dropped a penny and pretended to unthinkingly pick it up. I used my right hand, and felt relieved. By the time I got within a block of my house though, I was walking so fast I was almost running. I needed a pen and paper. It was ridiculous, I knew, yet no matter how many tests I devised for myself, nothing convinced me I was still right-handed.

I dropped the key trying to push it into the lock, then picked it up and turned it with my left hand. I scampered over to the phone where I kept a pen and notepad. "Mike Jefferies, Mike Jefferies," I printed over and over with my right, but each time it came out shaky and upwardly slanted. Cursive was impossible. Reluctantly, I switched to my left hand and in perfect script, wrote, "Mike Jefferies is right-handed."

*

Monday, I went into the office late. Big Brad lumbered toward me holding a cup of coffee. "Dude, sorry about Friday, Lil' Mike, I just . . ."

"Fuck off, Brad," I said, and I shoved him with my left hand. His coffee spilled on his white dress shirt.

"Duuuude!" he said.

I sat stewing at my desk for seven hours and left at four-thirty to find Miss Strange at the bar.

The place was nearly empty. The bartender leaned against the cash register and watched me pass. I sat in Miss Strange's booth.

The waitress came. "What can I get you?"

"Water," I said.

She tapped her pen against her notepad. "You waiting for someone then?" she asked.

"Yeah," I said.

She left reluctantly.

Miss Strange came through the door and flipped her sunglasses up so they rested on her untamed hair. In her left hand, she carried the Billy the Kid book. She saw me, smiled fiendishly, then walked toward me with a seductive, hippy swagger. I looked daggers at her, but watching her move, the way she floated toward me, I was seduced all over again. My nasty look faded the closer she came, and by the time she sat, I didn't know what to say.

She leaned across the table and whispered, "It's better, isn't it?"

"What did you do to me?" I said. The bite I'd been look-ing for was in my voice.

"Things are different now, right? They're better? More clear?"

"It's not natural. I mean, how did you . . ."

She couldn't stop smirking. "Look at this," she said, and she slapped her book on the table, pushed it toward me so it was upside down. "The gun smoke," she said. On the cover, there was an illustration of Billy crouched and firing his pistol. Gun smoke whirled above him. I remembered it from our last meeting, but this time when I looked at it, I saw the portrait of Billy repeated within the gray wisps of the smoke.

"You see it?"

"Yeah," I said.

"Didn't see it Friday, did you? Your right brain is work-ing now."

I started to understand. Sunday I'd laid in bed all day thinking, like my body needed to relearn everything. By the afternoon, I'd felt more comfortable than ever before.

"You drugged me. You took me home and drugged me," I said.

She giggled. "You needed it." She handed me two quar-ters. "Pick something," she said nodding to the jukebox.

I gave her a hard look. I wanted to be angry, but was more curious than anything.

"Go," she said.

Reluctantly, I went over to the jukebox and flipped through the pages. Someone had handwritten a small "(L)" next to certain songs. Joan Jett—I love Rock 'N Roll (L), Nirvana—Smells Like Teen Spirit (L), Dick Dale—Misirlou (L), Jimi Hendrix—Purple Haze (L). I knew she'd done it, that somehow she'd gotten behind that big glass bubble to denote all the famous left-handers, and it impressed me. Using my left hand, I dropped fifty cents into the jukebox. Jimi Hendrix started up. I walked back to my booth, sat, and smiled at Miss Strange. The song sounded better than I'd remembered. Miss Strange gave me a knowing nod. "That's what I mean," she said.

The waitress came by again. "What can I get you?"

I looked at Miss Strange. She shook her head. "Nothing," I said. "We're fine."

She set her hips off-kilter and gave a bounce. "Look, you're going to have to order something."

"Bring me that bowl of peanuts sitting on the bar," I said. Her eyes grew wide, and she walked away.

Miss Strange said, "Oooh. The new Mike. Good shootin', cowboy," and caressed my knee under the table.

I listened to Jimi wacking sounds out of his guitar. I pictured him on stage, head in the air, guitar turned upside down, coaxing out each electrified note with delicate aggression, his left hand moving quickly, powerfully. The guitar screamed. Billy the Kid was on stage with him too, slumped in a folding chair, squinting, daring anyone to rush the stage. Ty Cobb leaned on a speaker and grimaced at the crowd. He spat a stream of tobacco-laced saliva. Julius Caesar lay on a daybed off to the side of the stage. I stood in the front row with Miss Strange, her hair more scraggly than ever, and offered her the complimentary bowl of peanuts I held in my left hand. Jimi finished and let his strings vibrate and give off a slow fading sound, his left hand high in the air, and we all clapped. Caesar stood up on his bed. Billy the Kid smiled. Ty Cobb gave a cool wave. I noticed Mark Twain in the crowd too, stroking his handlebar mustache. We looked around at one another with approval. Brethren.

"I'm sorry. You're going to have to leave," the bar owner said. He was a middle-aged white guy with a mustache, presumably the manager, and he pointed at me with his right hand. He didn't know we were outlaws.

SONYA'S INSATIABLE HUNGER

I'd asked her not to go, but there she was, bouncing onstage on her toes, her head bobbing as she gulped down her forty-third hot dog. Five thousand raucous fans cheered. I knew she was counting bites—one, two, three, four—then a big swig of water, before swallowing it all down. She shoved in another dog. Her cheeks bulged like a chipmunk's. The crowd bellowed, "EAT! EAT! EAT!" in time with the digital clock's diminishing seconds. They all wanted the tiny Asian girl to outeat the twelve beefy men beside her. I tried to remain disaffected, but it was hard not to get caught up in it.

An ESPN camera loomed over her shoulder. A boom mic captured the sound of her chewing, her slurps of water in-between dogs. The broadcast lit up the JumboTrons around the stage. Sonya remained impervious to distraction. She watched the clock. Tracking her pace, I knew. Five hot dogs a minute would put her just shy of fifty-five, she'd said last week. I'd pretended I wasn't listening, that I still thought she'd bow out. If she beat that pace, stayed a fraction of a dog ahead, she'd take the record.

Fifty-two hot dogs at the nine-minute mark. Her jaw slowed. She put her hands to her belly but kept chewing, her pursed lips not quite closed. Bits of hot dog bun fell from her mouth onto the blue, plastic tablecloth. Her eyes narrowed, then bulged as she pushed the food down her throat with her tongue. Behind her, a blonde in a bikini held up a sign showing the number fifty-three. Fifteen dogs ahead of the closest competitor.

The emcee shouted, "She's closing in on a new record!"

Someone banged on a cowbell.

She swallowed her fifty-fourth dog and looked at the clock as she reached for another. Thirty seconds more, but after feeling in front of her with her hand, she looked down and noticed an empty tray. No dogs. She motioned to someone offstage. A Nathan's stagehand scurried about behind her. Ten seconds passed, and still she didn't have a hot dog.

The crowd started chanting her name: "SONYA! SONYA! SONYA!" A lone man broke the collective cheer by cupping his hands to his mouth and bellowing, "Bring her some fucking hot dogs!"

Fifteen seconds left. Sonya looked at the full plate of the opponent to her left. She grabbed a dog and wolfed it down. Fifty-five. The crowd boomed.

Sonya's burgled opponent, startled by the audience's outburst, looked over at her as she grabbed another, her fifty-sixth dog. He made a move with his elbow as if ready to fend her off, but stopped and instead tilted his body to grant her access.

The audience stood. Some still chanted her name. Others quieted in awe. Some had begun to count down the last ten seconds on the clock. The emcee screamed unintelligible sounds in a staccato rhythm into his microphone. Sonya put the record-setting dog into her mouth and chewed, chewed, chewed. Three, two, one . . . she took a swig of water and swallowed.

The buzzer sounded, and she pumped her fists in the air. The emcee grabbed her right hand and raised it high, almost yanking her off the ground. Flashbulbs. Cheering. Fireworks from backstage, and the crowd, in unison, chanted her name full force—"SONYA, SONYA, SONYA!" She wiped her mouth on her sleeve, and with the hot dog bun crumbs gone, looked instantaneously beautiful. Her opponents slumped in their chairs, drooped their heads over their fat necks, or walked offstage. Their hulking bodies accentuated the improbability of her feat.

"You've witnessed history! A new world record!" belted out the emcee. A Polo-shirted man emerged from backstage and placed an enormous gold crown on her head. It slid over her left eye. She righted it, maybe fiddled with it longer than she needed, knowing it played well for the cameras.

The Petite Princess of Pickles. The Madam of Meatballs. The Sexy Momma of Samosas. And now, the text below Sonya's image on the JumboTron proclaimed her the Diva of Dogs. A handsome ESPN reporter interviewed her onstage. Nathan's was the biggest contest in the world, and I knew it could be the victory that ruined us.

The crowd mostly gone, I stood among a few hundred

people watching as the reporter let his mic fall to his side, smiled at Sonya, and patted her on the back. She turned away, and her face fell. She placed her hands over her stomach, hunched, and shuffled backstage. I'd momentarily forgotten what she'd told me about how it feels afterwards. The bile collects in her esophagus. Bits of food keep coming into her mouth, and her stomach lurches, spasms, begging her to throw up.

I walked toward the side of the stage and saw the stagehands direct her toward the competitors' tent. A rope with attached sign reading "Employees Only" kept me away. The chatter of the emcee had given way to blaring pop music. Still, I could hear the sound of the competitors retching. I could distinguish Sonya from the rest.

I saw Dump Truck Doug, the construction worker from Chicago, come out of the tent, smile slightly, wipe his mouth, then put his arm around a pretty blonde. She patted his stomach, and they walked off together. A few other competitors emerged, plodding off like factory workers at the end of a shift.

Then, Sonya. I yelled to her.

She turned, and I saw the paleness of her smooth skin, the bags under her eyes. Absent of the radiance she'd shown for the cameras.

"You came," she said.

"Of course," I said, which was a stupid thing to say because I'd told her I wouldn't. "That was amazing."

She smiled and said, "I can't believe it." She came over to the rope, and I wanted to hug her, but knew I couldn't touch her, not until she'd finished digesting.

"No one can. They love you."

"What about you?"

"I'm so proud of you," I said. It was true, but I hated that she'd won.

She'd flown to New York because I'd refused to drive her. Nevertheless, she agreed to ride with me back to D.C. I helped her into the front seat. She reclined her chair and shut her eyes.

"Aaron?" she said, her eyes still closed and her face pointed toward the sun roof.

"Yeah?"

"Thanks for coming."

I feared she believed my presence was an apology, but I said, "Sure."

She wasn't asleep, but lay still. I watched her from the corner of my eye as I drove down 95. I could almost see her concentrating on her digestion, willing her body to quell the chaos in her stomach. She winced, squeezing her eyes tighter and accentuating the crow's feet. In less than two years, she'd be forty.

She fell asleep. I wished we could have talked during the drive to clear the air. Instead, I listened to CDs she wouldn't put up with while awake. I noticed the car making a grinding noise and was thankful that with

Sonya's prize money we could probably afford to fix it. She awoke when I exited 495 and headed into Silver Spring. I looked over at her, and she smiled back.

I slept on the couch. Sonya needed to sleep alone, soundly, and on her back. I wanted to press my body against hers, smell her, and receive silent assurance that things were okay. When she woke in the morning, she came to the couch where I lay reading a magazine and kissed me on my head.

"How are you feeling?" I asked.

"Good," she said. She walked over to the kitchen and poured a glass of milk. She took a prenatal vitamin out of the cupboard. This gave me hope, until she reached for the round disc that held her birth control pills. I sat up quickly, almost said something, then thought better of it. Let her have this moment, I told myself.

The prenatal vitamin, the doctor had said, was good preparation for pregnancy. This pissed me off. The first step toward pregnancy, I thought, was sex. Without contraceptives. Seeing Sonya swallow both pills was maddening. In a few days, I'd tell her so.

I walked to the phone and looked at the answering machine. I'd turned off the ringer when we arrived home the night before, and now there were fifty-two messages.

Sonya saw me and said, "How many?"

"Fifty-two."

She exhaled deeply. "Oh, Jesus," she said.

"Come on, Sonya. This is your favorite part."

She smiled. "Okay. It's not all bad. And it's great for the sport."

"And you look so much better on TV than Dump Truck Doug." I hugged her, ran my hand down her back to her ass. "How are you feeling?" I asked.

"Are you so concerned about me, or just wanting to know if I'm well enough to fuck?"

"Fucking is good for digestion, I read."

"Well, you should call Dump Truck Doug. He came away from that contest much worse off than I did."

"I'm not so concerned about Doug," I said. "But I'd really like to help you out." I kissed her on the neck right below her ear. She pushed her hair out of the way and led me to the bedroom. As I followed, I told myself how much I loved her, how half the guys in the audience yesterday were fantasizing about doing what I was about to, and how completely backwards it was for me, the man, to harbor a nagging frustration that the sex would be purely recreational.

Sonya spent most of the afternoon on the phone doing interviews and arranging appearances. I walked to Ellsworth Drive and picked up three burritos for her lunch and one for mine. I took my time about it, buying a soda, grabbing a freebie paper, and sitting on a bench for awhile. When I came back to the apartment, after I'd fiddled with the lock, Sonya stood in the middle of the living room with a wide grin on her face.

"What's with you?" I said.

"Want to go to New York tomorrow?"

"We just came from New York."

"New York City. Paid-for. Acela train tickets and a hotel right near Times Square."

"I've got work." Her grin faded into a slight smile. Wrong answer. "I can phone in."

"Good Morning America wants me. And you'll be in the studio too."

"Are you serious? That's fantastic," I said. I could tell she wanted me to be excited, but really, I didn't feel much like being Mr. Sonya Green. I wanted her to have her moment, not share it.

"And they want you tomorrow?"

"While the Nathan's win is still news." She hugged me tight around my neck, pulling me down to her. I wrapped my arms around her thin body.

"This is so great, Aaron."

"Yeah," I said.

An intern sat me in a chair behind the crew, and I watched them set up for the segment. Sonya stood with her arms raised as a sound engineer hooked a mic transmitter to the waistband of her miniskirt. After a lot of talk about the perfect outfit, Sonya had chosen the XXL T-shirt from the Nathan's contest, only rolled up at the arms and knotted in front to expose her midriff. A media-savvy dog diva, she knew to exploit her sex appeal and the peculiarity of her petite size.

The sound engineer finished and a slick guy in a suit, obviously her interviewer, talked with Sonya. She looked serious and nodded in response. A crewmember had placed a platter of hot dogs and a large cup of water on the table in front of her. In the background, hordes of tourists milled about with their trademark shout-out signs.

Then, the floor director, standing near me, yelled, "Thirty seconds." The crew scattered like cockroaches. The handsome man and Sonya stood smiling and looking at the camera, and the crowd behind them came alive with shouts and cheers.

"Ten, nine, eight," yelled the floor director. He signaled the final three numbers with his fingers, then pointed at the interviewer.

"We're live in Times Square with Sonya Green, Diva of Dogs, winner of the Nathan's Hot Dog Eating Contest and the $10,000 prize. Sonya, how many hot dogs did you eat?"

"I ate fifty-six hot dogs in ten minutes," she said.

"Woweee!" he said, rocking forward on his toes, his eyes bugging. He went on to ask the usual questions. They go something like this:

1) How do you stay so thin?
2) How do you prepare for a contest?
3) How did you get into competitive eating?

Sonya gave the usual answers, which go like this:

1)   I workout nearly four hours a day.

2)   I eat one large meal every day to train my stomach to expand.

3)   When I was in eighth grade, I challenged a boy to a pizza-eating contest in the cafeteria. I beat him, then went on to beat others, and found that I was pretty good at eating.

She used these prepared responses over and over and each sounded sincere. I disliked the answers. The TV-Sonya was simpler than the Sonya I knew.

The daily four-hour workout and long lunch doesn't leave time for a normal job. Sonya works part time at the front desk in our apartment building. She accepts packages from the UPS boy, makes sure guests sign the book, and buzzes in the pizza man. This, along with her prize money and a few endorsements, puts her annual income at about twenty thousand. There are also the costs of clothes, makeup for the appearances, and steep grocery bills. We'd spent over a hundred dollars on Nathan's Hot Dogs last month alone.

She'd challenged the eighth-grader to an eating contest out of desperation. He'd teased her relentlessly since sixth grade. He liked to lift the hem of her skirt, then, when she knocked his hand away, say, "I just want to know if it's true; if it's slanted like your eyes." Already knowing something of her talent, she'd asked him if he'd promise to leave her alone if she could outeat him. He'd made several lewd comments about how she could "eat him," then said, "I'll do your eating contest, Number Two," which was his nickname for her because she was pencil-thin with yellow skin.

The next morning she skipped breakfast and stole pizza money from her dad's wallet. At lunch, kids gathered around them and cheered as they ate. After she'd devoured all ten slices of her pizza, she looked up and wiped the tomato sauce off her face with the back of her hand. Those around watched in awestruck silence. Her nemesis stared at her too, then down at his remaining seven pizza slices. Someone yelled at him, "Fuck! You got schooled, Dan," and the kids started laughing. Someone else said, "Looks like Number Two is now Number One." Sonya carried the new nickname through graduation, taking down several challengers along the way.

Back in Times Square, the interviewer asked Sonya to eat as many hot dogs as she could in thirty seconds. She ate four, which was pretty amazing considering the early hour. Faster than her Nathan's pace. A sprint. She wiped up with a pink towel and listened as the interviewer exclaimed over her skill. Then, he said to her, "A lot of guys in the audience have noticed you're not wearing a wedding ring. Anyone special?"

"I'm just concentrating on competitive eating right now, training hard." She never wore her ring. She scored more endorsement money that way. Officially, I was okay with it.

"Well, I know a lot of the guys out there are going to be real interested in competitive eating from now on."

"Great," said Sonya. "The sport is growing. It's encouraging to see more and more people at these events each year."

"Thank you, Sonya," said the interviewer. Then, he stood smiling, frozen, staring at the camera until the director yelled, "clear." The masses in the background relaxed, and the crew came in to break down the table and remove the hot dog tray. The director shook Sonya's hand, showed her where I was, then pointed to the door leading into the studio. While walking alongside the crew, his mind was clearly on the next segment.

"You were great, Sonya," I said.

She smiled. "It was pretty fun, you know? Not competing, but just showing off."

"Yeah. You play great for the cameras. They want you for anything else?"

"Nah. We can get out of here. Just let me use the bathroom first."

"Okay. I'll wait here," I said.

Everyone assumed Sonya was bulimic, and I hated that she couldn't deny it. Lots of athletes are, according to Sonya, and not just in competitive eating—cross-country runners, wrestlers, all sports where discipline is paramount.

We got back on the train. Sonya looked out the window as we pulled out of Grand Central. She placed her hand on my knee, and I put my palm over hers. I listened to the rhythmic slap of the train's wheels against the track. The hoopla surrounding Sonya's win would diminish from here on out. There'd be other media attention, but nothing this big. Things would calm down, and we'd be left with each other and the argument. It would be a long ride home, and I knew I had to bring it up. I sat straighter. Sonya looked at me. Her face fell. She knew.

"Sonya, do you still want to have kids?"

"Yes. I've told you."

She turned from me to look at the backs of warehouses lining the train tracks.

"You're thirty-eight, Sonya."

No response. Then, she turned toward me. Her eyes narrowed, and she spoke in a flat voice. "Do you realize what you're asking me to do?"

"I'm asking you to start a family with me."

"I'm the best, Aaron."

"If there was any way to do both . . ."

"There isn't," she said.

"I know it's hard."

"What do you know? You've never been this good at anything. I wish you'd shut up about it," she said.

"That's low. Not fair." We talked through clenched jaws.

"You're goddamn right it's not," she said.

"Everything is about your eating. It's selfish. We're poor and childless."

She tightened her fists. In the past, she'd used a quiet,

almost apologetic tone when we had this discussion. After a moment, she said, "How about we go home, I'll throw out my birth control pills, and you fuck me until we procreate? I'll get a forty-hour-a-week job and start eating three meals a day. I'll get pregnant, gain weight, have a baby, stop training altogether, and sit in a cubicle while our kids go to daycare. Sound good?"

This sounded right to me, but Sonya talked like it was a nightmarish fairy tale. She turned to look out the window. I stared at my hands.

I thought of the first time I met her. I'd stopped for lunch at Three Brothers Pizza in Gaithersburg. A stage had been set up. Rows of seats faced it. The manager announced the Annual Pizza Eat-Off. Sonya came onstage, along with three other competitors. I'd been surprised to see a woman, and I'd stayed because she was beautiful. I'd fallen in love with her as she competed. The way her smile had faded seconds before the buzzer, the viciousness with which she'd attacked her pizza, how she'd wiped the red sauce from her face with her shirt sleeve, the way she'd punched the air when time ended and she realized she'd won.

I watched the back of her head, her straight black hair resting on her shoulders.

I knew what I had to say, and I knew I had to say it when Sonya couldn't see how my face betrayed my words.

"Sonya, maybe we don't have to have kids. There are other ways to be happy."

"Maybe," she said, still facing the window. "But I don't want that either." She turned to me with tears on her cheeks and leaned toward me. I held her and stroked her hair. Her thin body bobbed in rhythm with her silent sobs. Resting my chin on top of her head, I watched the simple houses and worn water tower of a New Jersey suburb pass. I knew that tomorrow we'd wake in our one-bedroom apartment. Before breakfast, Sonya would go to the cupboard, take out her prenatal vitamin and her birth control pill, and swallow them both. I would do my best not to say anything.

ACKNOWLEDGMENTS

When writing, I'm usually trying to impress my wife Elizabeth who, surprisingly, is able to offer some pretty honest critiques despite her undying love for me. She is my first reader, toughest critic, and biggest supporter. She makes me a better writer and a more well-adjusted human being.

My friend and fellow writer Jeremy Trylch read every story in this book several times, and helped improve them with each reading. I'm grateful for his hard work and friendship.

My mother, author and illustrator Alice Carter, read and edited many of these stories in early drafts as did Marlene Strauss. Alice Carter and Courtney Granner are also responsible for the phenomenal cover of this book.

Thanks to Mark Farrington, Richard Peabody, and Margaret Meyers at The Johns Hopkins University. Their passion for storytelling made me a better reader and writer. I'm thankful I found them and glad they are giving others the education I received.

Family and friends who deserve thanks and who are depicted in this book more than they know include: Robert Carter, Amanda LeNay, Dennis Carter, Jane Eisenstat, Benjamin Eisenstat, Jeff Austin, and Todd Liu.

Thanks to the people who have published and critiqued my work, including Zachary Benavidez, Bob Callaci,

Kevin Colligan, Brietta Forbes, Brian J. Hatcher, Dave Housley, Cathy Irwin, Matt Kirkpatrick, Colin Meldrum, Clair Nixon, Neil Ellis Orts, Richard Peabody, Katherine Sanger, Grant Tracey, Julie Wakeman-Lin.

Erin McKnight and others at Queen's Ferry Press worked tirelessly to improve this text and to form it into a cohesive, clean product.

Lastly, getting to know my kids, Benjamin and Brett Carter, has been wonderfully fascinating. I look forward to the day I can share these stories with them without anyone feeling uncomfortable about Daddy's use of four-letter words.

ABOUT THE AUTHOR

Theodore Carter is the author of The Life Story of a Chilean Sea Blob and Other Matters of Importance, Frida Sex Dreams and Other Unnerving Disruptions, and Stealing 'The Scream'. He's appeared in several magazines and anthologies including The North American Review, Pank, Necessary Fiction, A capella Zoo, The Potomac Review, and Gargoyle.

Carter's street art has garnered attention from several local news outlets including The Washington Post, NBC4 Washington, Fox5 DC, and the Washington City Paper. He's created commissioned murals and sculptures for local businesses and for Washington D.C.'s Art All Night. In 2019, Carter organized the Night of 1,000 Fridas and helped make 1,000 pieces of Frida Kahlo-inspired art accessible to the public on the same night. Connect online:

www.theodorecarter.com
Instagram: @theodorecarter2
Twitter: @theodorecarter2
Facebook: @chileanseablob

www.ingramcontent.com/pod-product-compliance
Lightning Source LLC
Chambersburg PA
CBHW050302110726
47898CB00007B/2503